PARADISE LANE
By Fran McNabb

Copyright © 2019 Fran McNabb
Published by: Take Me Away Books, an imprint of Winged Publications

This book is a work of fiction. Names, characters, places, and incidents are the product of the author's imagination and are used fictitiously. Any resemblance to actual events, locales, or persons, living or dead, is coincidental.

No part of this book may be copied or distributed without the author's consent.

All rights reserved.

ISBN-13: 979-8-8689-1286-3

DEDICATION:

To: Diane Sicuro for her friendship, help, and support. Old friends are the best.

ACKNOWLEGEMENTS:

Writing is a solitary endeavor, but sometimes an author needs help. Special thanks go to Diane Sicuro, Sue Gallaspy, and CaraLynn James for once again coming to the aide of an old friend. You have my deepest affection and gratitude.

Chapter One

The Yellow Rooster would have to wait.

Slade Larson never wasted time, but his restaurant wasn't going anywhere. He stood on the newly built boardwalk running along Biloxi's Back Bay. Its calm waters washed away the last two hectic decades, and he was once again a young man living the carefree life along the Gulf Coast. Here is where he and his brother had played and fished, where he had taken high school girls on his small skiff, and where he floated alone when he had to get away from the yelling between his parents.

The channel at this spot in the bay was narrow, but the memories he had here could wrap around the world and back.

He picked up a pebble and threw it, but instead of skipping across the water, it sank.

Slade laughed. "I guess I'm a little rusty."

He turned away from the bay and headed toward his restaurant. Instead of hurrying to make up for his daydreaming, he took his time as he walked past the businesses that had opened since he'd last been home. A small marina, a souvenir shop, an ice cream parlor, a bakery, and several buildings under construction were pumping life into the once dead bay road of Paradise Lane.

He wished Slade's Seafood Restaurant, the family business that his brother Mac was still running, was on this up-and-coming road. At one time the restaurant was the hot spot, but now Mac was having trouble. Even though Slade was a still a partner on paper, he'd left the area years ago to start an investment business in New York, but when Mac asked for his help, he wasted no time in flying to the coast.

Now seeing how Paradise Lane was pulling in attractive businesses, he wondered if he'd be able to help his brother.

He headed toward The Yellow Rooster, the restaurant his investment company had acquired not too long ago. Situated in the middle of this new tourist strip, the business had been a good buy. As he got nearer to the building, the well-kept, clean exterior and manicured greenery told him he'd done well when he hired Gary Morton as his manager and gave him a small share of the business.

"Is Gary in?" Slade asked a young man unloading boxes of paper products just inside the side door.

"Yes, sir. He's in the office."

He thanked him, then walked through another door and entered a dimly lit dining area with new tables and chairs, upbeat, modern décor and a bandstand that would make his brother drool.

With a quick knock he entered the office. "Gary,

you have a minute?

His manager sat behind an older mahogany desk bent over a stack of paperwork. When he looked up and recognized Slade, he stood up. "I heard you were on the coast. I wondered if you'd actually show your face around here."

"You didn't think I'd be here and not come see our place?"

Gary walked around the desk and the two men shook hands.

"I'm here to give my brother a hand at Slade's and to see for myself how The Yellow Rooster is looking." Slade held onto the man's hand a little longer than necessary. "And to let you know how much I appreciate all you've done down here. I have to tell you how impressed I am with the place. It doesn't even look like the same building."

"Your partner is doing pretty darned good, but I guess you felt the need to come check up on me." The man laughed.

"No, Gary. If I didn't trust you to run this place right, you wouldn't be here."

"Yeah. I kind of realized that the day we signed papers."

"I have to say the restaurant, lounge, and bandstand look great. You have good taste, and I love the sign out front. That artist you recommended does great work. It's exactly what I envisioned."

Gary pulled out a chair and straddled it.

Slade sat in one near the desk.

"So you're here to help Mac," Gary said. "I hear he's having a hard time lately. I'm sure he could use your advice."

"I don't know if I have the kind of advice that can keep that place open. It's in worse shape than I thought."

"That's not good, but if anyone can turn the business around, you can. Are you thinking about buying his share and doing the business right?"

Slade shook his head. "I couldn't do that to my brother. He's just like my dad. That restaurant is his life. I'd hate to see it go under like so many others do and have to sell for pennies on the dollar."

"May I remind you that's how you got The Yellow Rooster?"

"Yeah, I do remember. Good for me, but bad for the last owner." Slade inhaled deeply. "I'll try my best to get Mac on his feet and then cross my fingers."

"I understand," said Gary as he stretched. "Now what can I do for you?"

The two men talked about the business. Slade was impressed and wished he could spend more time here, but he stood up. "I really have to go. I'm trying to keep a low profile around Mac when it comes to The Yellow Rooster. He's still angry I bought the place."

"I can see where he'd be upset, but how did you know this place would start a tourist phenomenon on the bay?"

"Yeah, what's the old saying, 'the best laid plans. . .' I was buying this place for a quick flip, not to create competition for anyone. Who knew you'd make it into the talk of the town?"

"I'm not apologizing for doing a good job," Gary threw in.

"No, I'm pleased with everything you've done. It simply wasn't in my plans to keep it this long or to start drawing the tourists here instead of up the road by Mac's place."

"As I said, I won't apologize for making this place what it is, but I will say I'm sorry I don't have the money yet to buy you out like we talked about."

"We're good, Gary. My word is good." Slade stood up. "I'll hang onto my share until you can swing the deal."

"I hate it's giving more fuel for Mac's anger."

"I'm dealing with him. He's my brother and we love each other, no matter how mad we get."

Gary walked Slade to the front door. Slade looked out at the small family-style café across the street. "How's that restaurant doing? Is it holding its ground?"

"I'm not so sure," Gary said. "Since The Yellow Rooster opened, I have a feeling we're taking away some of her business. I hear the owner is struggling."

"Hmmm, maybe I need to make an offer on that business as well."

"You don't know, do you?"

Slade looked at his partner and shook his head.

"Slade, the owner is the widow you bought this place from. Both of these buildings were her husband's, but she hung onto the smaller one and is trying to keep it open. From what I hear, she's having a rough go of it, and to top things off, she has a sick little girl."

"What?"

"Yeah," Gary said. "I didn't know about her owning it either until I started living most of my life here at the restaurant. Sweet lady. I've been over several times. Good home cooking but not exactly a tourist draw."

Slade rubbed his hand across his chin. "I had no idea. I thought the money she got from the sale of this place would set her up."

"From what I've heard her husband left her with huge debts."

The air left Slade's chest. "I think I'll walk over there to check the place out and grab a bite."

"I'm sure she'll appreciate your business." Gary unlocked the front door, then turned to Slade. "Does she know you own this place?"

"Part-owner."

"Semantics, my friend. Semantics."

"I don't know if she does or not. I never met her in person. When I bought the place, I had my attorney down here work with her. I knew the building and didn't feel the need to come down. The building was bought by the investment company, not me per se. I don't know that anyone but Mac associates me with my company, and I don't think he says much about it since he hates the fact I'm up there and he's down here."

"I hope you and Mac can come to terms about everything, and I hope you can save his restaurant."

"Thanks, Gary."

Slade crossed the narrow street. The bell above the door dinged as he entered the small dining room. Three booths lined one wall and only four small tables stood in the center. On each table was a tiny vase with pink flowers in them. As he passed the first table, he realized the flowers were real.

Nice touch.

As he took his seat on a barstool at the counter, a lady swung open the door to the kitchen. "I'm so sorry. I heard the bell, but I was talking with my cook." She greeted him with a warm, beautiful smile.

"No problem. I just got seated."

She placed a menu in front of him, then took his drink order. While she filled his glass, he looked at her closely. Maybe in her early thirties with long dark blond hair pulled back and tied with a simple pink ribbon, she wasn't a standout beauty, but something about her was natural and refreshing and just plain cute. When he realized she was turning around with his drink, he looked down at the menu, a one-page list with a few appetizers, sandwiches, and specials for each day of the week.

"Here we go." She placed the cola in front of him, but her smile was gone. "Do you need more time to decide?"

"Nope, that shrimp salad sounds great." He looked up from the menu and studied her face. Something was familiar about her.

"I have to brag about the salad. It was my mother's recipe and it's a favorite here."

She hung the order on a spinning holder above an opening in the wall. When no one took it down, she excused herself and walked through the kitchen door.

When she came out a few minutes later, she smiled. "I'm sorry. My day cook is pretty new and is still learning the ropes, but don't worry he's a coast boy and does a great job with Mom's salad."

"It's fine. I know how hard it is to get and keep good help. My brother and I have a restaurant not far from here"

He was about to tell her he was also the co-owner of The Yellow Rooster, but she cut him off in a tone that made him sit up straight.

"I know who you are. You're Slade Larson, Mac's brother."

Slade stared at this attractive woman. Had he met her before, he would've remembered, but then another thought struck. *Does she know I own New York Investments?*

"Have we met?"

"You don't remember, do you?" She straightened her shoulders. "We went to high school together."

Slade was never lost for words, but at the moment he had trouble finding his voice. "High school? Here in Marsh Isles?"

"Yep. You were one year ahead of me. We didn't run in the same crowd, but I remember you. You were one of the jocks—uh, you played sports," she corrected herself and smiled, but it wasn't a sweet smile.

Her reference to him as a jock hurt. Yes, playing sports was his life back then, but what was wrong with that? His teammates were good guys, or at least that's the way he remembered them. "I'm so sorry. What was your maiden name?"

"I was a Seymour. Nicole Seymour. I'm now Nicole Russo."

He knew her present name. Even though he hadn't come face-to-face with her, he never forgot the owners of the businesses he acquired.

"Nicole, I'm so sorry I didn't recognize you. My memories are vague from those high school years. I guess you had to be running with a football for me to remember your name." His words were meant to be a joke, but Nicole didn't smile.

The bell dinged at the food window. Without comment, she turned, picked up the order and placed it in front of Slade. "Enjoy. If you need something, don't hesitate to call."

Slade was dumbfounded. What happened to the sweet smile and happy-go-lucky girl who greeted him when he first came in? Had he done something to her in high school or did she just dislike jocks in general?

He tasted his shrimp salad and had to agree with her. It was wonderful. The one they served at Slade's wasn't nearly this good.

"Nicole, this is delicious. I might have to send Mac down here to see what he's doing wrong with his salad."

She looked up from a stack of receipts. "I like Mac. I'd love to show him how to make it. Do you cook when you're at the restaurant?"

At least she was trying to have a decent conversation. "No, not now. I used to share all the responsibilities with him when I lived here, but now I'm part of the business in name only. I'm here only to give him some advice."

"Then you have the good side of the ownership. I own, cook, run and clean this place." She laughed softly.

Her laugh made Slade smile. Maybe she was warming up to him.

"Guess you could call me a one-girl operation," she continued. "I do have someone in the kitchen to help during the lunch and dinner hours, but except for that, what you see is what you get."

This time her smile reached all the way to her eyes. Her love for this little café was genuine.

"I'm impressed," Slade said, but in the back of his mind, he knew the meaning behind her words. There wasn't enough money to hire people to give her the backup she needed. Seemed she was in the same boat

Mac was in. He wanted The Yellow Rooster to succeed, but not at the expense of small businesses like hers or the older establishments like his brother's.

She went back to her paperwork, but immediately looked up when the kitchen door flew opened. A little girl with long black hair bounced in and waved to him.

"Hi, I'm Em. What's your name?"

Nicole bent down, probably telling her not to speak to the customers before Slade could answer.

"It's okay, Nicole. I'd love to talk to your little girl if you don't mind."

Nicole looked at him then at Em, then nodded. She whispered something to her daughter, but Slade couldn't hear.

Em walked around the counter. Slade stuck out his hand. "Hi, Em. My name is Mr. Slade."

"Hi, Mr. Slade. Do you live around here?"

"I used to. In fact, I went to school with your mother."

Em wrinkled her nose. "You went to school when you were little?"

"Yep, I did," Slade smiled then looked at Nicole who was also smiling.

"Why don't you live here now?"

Slade pulled his attention back to Em. "My work is in another state, but my brother lives here and he also has a restaurant like your mom does."

Nicole spoke up. "Em, you know his brother. It's Mr. Mac."

"I like Mr. Mac. He comes down here sometimes and eats what my mama cooks."

"Em, let's let Mr. Slade eat in peace. Why don't you go back in the kitchen until Miss Tillie comes to get you?"

"Oh, do I have to?"

Nicole smiled but then gave her daughter a firm look.

"Okay." Em turned back to Slade. "Miss Tillie is like my grandma. I love her and she loves me."

"You're one lucky girl if you have someone to love you like that."

Em spun around and skipped into the kitchen.

"Nicole, your daughter is beautiful and very personable. Thank you for letting her talk to me."

"I try to keep her away from the café, but Miss Tillie had an appointment this morning. I hope she didn't bother you."

"Absolutely not. I'm not around children much, and it's refreshing to talk with them. We adults could learn a lot from them if we just stopped our hectic lives and gave them a chance."

The smile that Nicole gave him warmed his heart "Thank you for sharing that. That's pretty deep for a jock." She laughed then turned into the kitchen.00000

Slade chuckled and decided he really hoped he'd get to see her again. He took another bite, but he had a hard time enjoying his food. He couldn't get his mind off the fact that he was the one who had paid pennies on the dollar to buy her restaurant across the street. Now, according to Gary, she might end up losing this one as well.

He had not made a very good first impression on her since she only remembered him as a jock. Whether she knew he now owned her husband's restaurant or not, he didn't want to give her anything else to dislike about him. He wasn't going to be on the coast long, but there was something about her that made him want her to like him.

Grow up, Slade.

Slade liked a challenge, but he was afraid she'd never warm up to him.

As he ate, Nicole got up from her paperwork, went in and out of the kitchen carrying clean plates and glasses. She wiped down countertops, answered the phone, and went back through her stack of papers. She even found time to check to make sure he didn't need anything.

When he finished, he paid his bill, left her a really nice tip, then quickly headed out. He needed fresh air. She thanked him, but didn't bother to say it was nice seeing him or anything else that would've made him feel welcomed in her café.

He left the café feeling terrible. As long as he lived his life in New York, the problems here in this little coastal town didn't take up much of his day, in fact, he barely thought about what went on down here. Now that he'd seen the struggles Mac was having with the restaurant and the plight of the widow from whom he'd bought the business, he knew it would be hard to return to his world of big business, high finance, and luxury living without thinking about this little spot on the coast.

He turned onto the sidewalk, glancing once more through the window of the café. Nicole was bending over one of tables but looked up as he passed. For a brief moment their gazes connected.

He nodded and continued walking as if her expression had not pierced his heart. Her happy-go-lucky smile was gone. In its place was sadness and heartache.

Slade kept walking, but he had a strong urge to run back in and protect her from what life had thrown at her—from what *he* had thrown at her.

Nicole Russo was a stranger to him, but could he push her image away?

~

Nicole pulled her gaze away from Slade and tried to concentrate on the table she was wiping down. She breathed easier as he walked beyond the window of her café.

She stood up straighter and stared at the empty sidewalk.

Slade Larson. Of all people to walk into her café.

The best athlete in Marsh Isles High School. The most popular and gorgeous guy in the halls. The most everything including all-round jock, which to her and her small group of nerdy friends was not something to be desired.

Yeah right.

Nicole swiped the cloth across the table one last time, then headed to the kitchen. In the back of her mind she knew everyone in her group wanted to be like them and the cheerleader-type they ran with.

She laughed. The man was still gorgeous, even more than when he was as a teenager, but she had a feeling he hadn't gotten rid of the jock, better-than-thou attitude from years ago.

Of course, he did seem pleasant today, and she loved the way he interacted with Em. He probably didn't even remember how she'd been the brunt of some of the football players' hurtful pranks, but that really didn't matter.

Knowing she'd probably never run into him again, she pushed the thought of Slade Larson aside.

She had a café to run and a little girl who depended on her. Even though her small business would never be as attractive as The Yellow Rooster and some of the other new businesses going up on the street, she knew the food she served was excellent. It made her feel good to watch her small following of locals enjoy the meals she served.

She pushed through the swinging doors of the kitchen to check on Em and to get ready for her lunch clientele, but not before glancing at the empty sidewalk once more.

Would she ever see Slade Larson again?

Chapter Two

Nicole backed her twelve-year-old Jeep from behind her café, then turned north as she made her way toward Bluebird Drive where she'd lived most of her life. Even though her street sat just a few blocks from Paradise Lane with all its new businesses, she rarely passed another car in her neighborhood. Most cars stayed south of the bay that separated Marsh Isles from the tourist district near the beachfront. She liked it that way.

Bungalows and cottages with inviting front porches and nicely kept yards lined the narrow winding roads. Several ladies working in their flower beds looked up and waved. Nicole waved back. She loved the welcoming feeling of coming home each day to neighbors who knew her and neighborhoods that were filled with families who had lived in the same houses for many years.

Nicole didn't mind the winding road. Her Jeep's small size allowed her to maneuver these older streets much better than a normal size car, but in her heart she knew that wasn't the reason she kept a vehicle that was so impractical for a parent to drive. She and Tony had bought the vehicle when they'd moved back to the coast. Tony called it his toy on wheels. It was his pride and joy, washing it regularly with the garden hose. She could still see him dancing around the vehicle and singing, sometimes with the neighbors cheering him on.

Those memories kept him close to her heart, and she simply wasn't ready to get rid of the Jeep just for something more practical. Sitting on its cracked leather seat and letting the warm southern breeze blow through her hair still connected her to her late husband.

Rubbing her hand along the steering wheel, she took a moment to get rid of the loneliness she fought when the problems of the world weighed heavy on her shoulders. When he had been alive, Tony created more problems than he solved, but having him with her had made the problems easier to face.

Not wanting to add any more to her stress, she pushed aside thoughts of Tony. She always made sure she had a smile on her face for her daughter when she came home from the é. She turned east onto Bluebird Drive then pulled into her driveway.

She grabbed her purse then without thinking reached toward the back seat for her guitar case. Immediately she jerked her arm back. Why had she done that? It had been years since she and Tony made a living singing together. They'd played as a team at Slade's Seafood Restaurant and then in their own restaurant. It was their music that brought in more money than the food.

Many of her friends and family thought singing at

restaurants and lounges was below her degree in music, but Nicole never looked at their gigs that way. She loved singing and playing, no matter the venue. Even though she'd traded in her singing gigs to be a café owner, she still gave piano and guitar lessons to help supplement that income and now worked with the church choir. But, playing gigs alone? Never. She looked at the empty seat where her guitar case once sat, then headed to the front of her house to see Miss Tillie and Em.

Mrs. Mildred Mason, or Miss Tillie as everyone called her, was Nicole's neighbor, best friend, substitute mother for her and substitute grandmother for Emily, and an all-round lifesaver since Tony's death. Her curly white hair, her starched and ironed blouses, and comfortable shoes always gave Nicole an at-home-loving feeling, and today she needed all of that.

She walked alongside her cottage that had been in her mother's family for several generations. When her mother remarried and moved to Tennessee, she gave the house to Tony and Nicole with the stipulation that it always had to remain in the family. That was fine with Nicole, and Tony loved being part of the rich culture along the Gulf Coast. Every day she felt thankful to live here and to raise her daughter.

As she headed to the front of her cottage, she wiped away the pity party she'd had on her ride home. Seeing Miss Tillie sitting in the front porch rocker brought a smile to her face. Except for her daughter's beautiful smile and big hugs, Miss Tillie's welcome took away any misery she'd had at work or the melancholy she felt when she'd walk into an empty house. Without Tony's welcoming arms, it was hard to step into their house, but Miss Tillie made life bearable for her.

She greeted Miss Tillie then looked around for her daughter. "Is Emily already in bed?"

"Yes. She had a good day, but she was tired and went to her room early."

"Is she feeling okay?"

"She's fine. I just checked on her and she's asleep already. She drew some pictures for you, but they can wait until tomorrow. Dinner is on the stove."

"I was hoping to get a few hugs from her tonight." Nicole stood still letting the day's problems come crashing down on her.

Miss Tillie stood up, opened her arms and pulled Nicole into a big bear hug. "What's wrong?" She held Nicole close and rubbed her hands down her back. "Did you have a bad day?"

Nicole placed her head on the lady's shoulder and fought to keep the tears from rolling down her cheek. Finally she inhaled deeply, then blew out a big breath. For several minutes she relished the soft protection of the lady's body and the smell of dinner still clinging to her clothes.

Finally Miss Tillie held her at arm's length. "Were some of your customers rude? There's no excuse for people to disrespect anyone trying to make a living."

Nicole inhaled a ragged breath, then pulled out a used tissue from her pocket to wipe her nose. "No, Miss Tillie, none of the customers said anything to me. In fact, it was a rather quiet day. It seems as though my dinner crowd gets smaller every day."

"Things will pick up. They always do."

"They do for The Yellow Rooster. I'm not sure how I can compete."

"You keep serving those delicious meals and you won't have to worry." Miss Tillie looked at her closer. "Is something else bothering you?"

Nicole chuckled and took a seat in one of her porch rockers. "I had someone come in today from my high school years. I think all the insecurities I felt back then came rushing back to me."

Miss Tillie sat next to her. "Insecurities? You? Why, you are the most confident, beautiful young lady I know."

Again Nicole smiled. "You're much too sweet. I can assure you I wasn't always confident. I was really shy and klutzy in high school, except when I was singing. Once I'd make myself open my mouth, I'd forget everything around me and just sing. I loved it."

"And everyone now loves the way you sing. So, who made you dredge up those insecurities?"

"Mac Larson's brother."

"His brother? Do you mean Slade?"

Nicole wiped her nose. "You know Mac's brother?"

"Not really know him, but I met him years ago. When my husband had the tour business, we worked with all of the businesses on the Biloxi strip. When Mr. Larson opened his restaurant back here, we started driving the passengers across the bay bridge to see some of the sights in Marsh Isles. We'd always let them stop at the restaurant so it was his father, the first Mr. Slade, who was my husband's friend. He opened the restaurant and kept a good business until he died about six or seven years later. That's when the two sons took over, but that partnership didn't last long. I'm not sure what happened, but Slade left the coast." Miss Tillie fanned herself. "Their father was such a nice gentleman."

"How did Mr. Larson die?"

"Heart attack. Died right at the register before an ambulance could get to him. Real sad, it was."

"I'm sure it was." She thought a minute about the two brothers trying to make a success of their father's business. "I don't remember those years. I was in college in New York. Then I got married and, well, you know how busy those early years in a marriage are."

"Busy but oh so happy." Miss Tillie touched Nicole's arm.

Nicole took a deep breath and thought about the Larson brothers. "So the boys took over the business."

"Yes, but then my Henry got sick and had to give up the tour company. I lost track of what went on down around the tourist area. Even after Henry died, I didn't venture into that neighborhood anymore. I'm perfectly content to sit here on our little street and watch the world go by from my front porch swing."

Nicole understood. She and Tony had moved back to her hometown about seven years ago, and this is where she wanted to raise Em. One day she'd have to go someplace else temporarily for Emily to have more specialized treatments for her blood disease, but her hope was to return here to live. She prayed the café provided enough income to continue doing just that.

"So how is Slade?" Miss Tillie asked. "He was such a good looking young man. I'm sure he grew into quite a handsome adult."

"I guess."

"You guess?" Miss Tillie laughed.

"Well, yes, he's still handsome." Now it was Nicole's turn to laugh. "He didn't even remember me from our high school years."

"If he didn't know you then and doesn't remember you now, it's his misfortune."

"You're good for my ego, Miss Tillie. Thank you."

Miss Tillie stood up. "Your ego is just fine. I'll see you tomorrow."

"Thanks. I don't know what I'd do without you. You're a godsend for Emily and me."

She laughed. "You and Emily are like family to me." She laughed. "Anyway, what else do I have to do?" With a wave she left Nicole sitting on the porch and walked down the sidewalk toward her house, stopping to talk with several other ladies who sat on their porches enjoying the early evening.

Eager to check on Emily, Nicole got up from her chair and went inside the quiet house. After placing her purse on a small hall table, she headed to her daughter's room.

Stepping close to the bed, Nicole ran her hand down the black curls spread out on the pillow. Emily had inherited Tony's dark traits. She was beautiful as a little girl and would be a stunning young lady one day.

She wished Tony were here to watch her grow. He'd be so proud. She bent over and kissed her on the forehead, then went to the hall phone to check her messages. She wanted to get rid of her land line, but so many of Tony's old colleagues in the music industry and her family had this number so she held onto it.

The message light blinked. Nicole hoped it was her mother. She could use her cheerful voice, but when she hit the button the gruff voice of Barry Keats filled the room. She took a step back, bit her lip, and stared at the recorder as Barry reminded her that her note was past due again. It was the last thing Nicole needed to hear tonight.

When the message ended, Nicole stood in the hallway unmoving. She raised her eyes to heaven and prayed. She didn't know where to turn to pay off the debts Tony had left her.

Nicole had never met Barry while Tony was alive, but she knew him now. She and Tony had gotten a loan from a local bank to buy two properties on Paradise Lane, but, without telling Nicole, he'd also gotten a loan from Barry. When Tony died without life insurance, she had no choice but to sell the one building now called The Yellow Rooster to a New York acquisitions company. It was either sell to them or lose the building. With the little money she received, she paid off the bank, remodeled the smaller building across the street for her café, put some into savings, and thought things were okay.

But then she met Barry. He knocked on her door one evening, explaining she needed to pay off the loan. He looked like an understanding man, but he made it clear he needed his money.

That evening she'd stood in the door, not knowing what to say. At first she questioned his demand. How could Tony owe this man?

Barry was prepared. He pulled out a stack of papers, which were signed by Tony and notarized. "Mrs. Russo, I'm sorry you didn't know about this loan, but I gave your husband the money with his assurance I'd be paid within two years. He only made a few small payments and now I need my money. I've been patient long enough."

"I understand, but you have to give me a little time.

Would you consider some sort of payment plan? That would be easier for me rather than lump sums."

They came up with a plan that was much more than Nicole could afford, but it was the only plan he approved of.

Now it was time to pay the next big installment.

She had never been behind on a payment in her life, and now she was over her head. What could she do? There was no more money.

She twisted her hands, then hit the delete button.

The second message made her smile. It was her mother's sweet voice. Just as in all their telephone conversations, she begged Nicole to come home with Emily for good or at least for a visit before school started.

Nicole wished she could feel her mom's arms around her, but that wasn't possible now or anywhere in the near future. Leaving Marsh Isles and living with them in Tennessee wasn't an option either. Her mother and stepdad lived in a small house and barely made ends meet. Having Nicole and Emily with them wouldn't help their situation, and their location away from any big cities and medical communities was out of the question. Emily needed close contact with her local doctors.

At least here on the coast, Nicole had her own home with no house payments and a pediatrician who knew Emily and closely watched over her. Even so, Dr. Murry and the blood specialist to whom he'd referred Emily had made it clear one day she'd have to find a hospital where Em could receive treatments.

Their words were always on her mind.

She didn't bother to call her mother back even

though talking with her would make her feel better. She hit the message delete button, then headed for the shower.

How could she talk with her mom knowing her business wasn't doing well and Barry Keats was demanding payment of his loan?

She needed a warm shower to wash away her worries.

~

The next morning Emily crawled into bed and cuddled next to her.

"Good morning, Sweetie." Nicole kissed the top of her head.

Emily giggled. "I thought you were asleep."

"Nope, not with my big girl next to me." She rolled to her side and gave Emily a big hug.

"I fell asleep before you got home. Miss Tillie said you'd wake me to tell me goodnight, but you didn't."

Nicole stretched and put her arm behind her head. "You're right. I didn't want to wake you, but I did kiss you and tell you goodnight. You know I could never sleep without our kisses."

Emily giggled again. "What're we doing today? Miss Tillie said I didn't have school again."

"That's right. It's Sunday. We'll go to church then to breakfast. How would you like to go to the beach or park before my students start coming in?"

"Yay. I love the beach. Can we swim?"

"We'll see. I'm not sure we have time to do that. I have students a little later." Nicole knew there was time for her daughter to swim, but with her health, Nicole didn't take any chances in the water.

"Olivia said she went swimming last week."

"We'll see. Miss Tillie has a friend with a pool. Maybe she'll let us play in it one day this week."

"Okay."

Emily slid out of bed without arguing. *How do I deserve such a little angel?*

"Come on, Mama. I'm hungry."

Nicole rolled out of bed. "We'll eat a light breakfast so we can go to the restaurant with Miss Tillie after church. She likes our little outings."

After breakfast, Nicole dressed Emily in a pink dress with silver shoes and white socks with lace on the tops.

Emily stood in front of the mirror. "This is my favorite dress, Mama. I love it."

Nicole pulled out a brush from the dresser drawer. "You say that every morning with every dress you wear, Sweetie."

"All my dresses are my favorites."

Nicole loved brushing her daughter's hair. Thick and black and shiny, Emily's hair was Tony's pride and joy. How he'd love to help brush it now that it was longer and thicker.

With a large pink bow at the back of her head, Emily spun around and laughed.

"Let's go," Nicole said. "Miss Tillie will be waiting for us."

"She always goes to church with us, huh?"

"Yes, she does and we're so lucky she wants to be with us."

"She's like my grandma."

Nicole helped Emily into the tiny back seat of the Jeep. "You can call her your grandmother if you'd like. I know that makes her happy." Nicole thought how sad it was that her daughter didn't remember Tony's parents or her mother. She hoped one day she could remedy that situation.

Miss Tillie was already walking toward the car when Nicole pulled up to the curb. "What a wonderful day for our beautiful girl in pink."

"That's me, huh?"

"It certainly is."

Just as on most Sundays, the three of them attended church where Nicole played the organ and sang with the choir. Afterwards they drove across the bay bridge to a part of old Biloxi called The Point to eat at a small restaurant overlooking the water. Behind the restaurant a long pier lined with charter boats and shrimp boats stretched out into the Mississippi Sound. Sometimes the three of them walked on the pier after their breakfast so Em could watch the fishermen unload their catch. This morning there wasn't a cloud in the sky and Nicole looked forward to their walk.

Nicole took Em's hand and headed for the restaurant. The hostess recognized Em and Nicole and talked to Em as she led them to a table next to a big window.

As soon as they ordered, Nicole groaned. Slade Larson entered the restaurant, greeted the hostess with a devastating smile, and sat at a table not too far from them. He didn't look in their direction so Nicole assumed he had not seen them.

After the waitress took their orders, Nicole dared look in Slade's direction. He caught her eye and nodded.

She nodded back, then turned her attention to adding sweetener to her coffee.

Emily looked at the man then at her mother and waved. "Look, Mama, that's Mr. Slade. Remember him? He's waving back."

Nicole groaned again. She didn't want to wave to the man who made her remember the high school years she struggled through.

"Mama, wave back."

"Do you know him?" asked Miss Tillie.

"That's Slade Larson."

"Ooh. I thought he looked familiar." Miss Tillie patted her chest with her hand. "He's grown into quite a handsome man."

"I hadn't noticed."

Now Miss Tillie laughed out loud.

Nicole raised her hand and waved a little, then tried to turn the conversation with Miss Tillie away from Slade, but as she talked she realized Emily kept looking at Slade and making funny faces. As hard as she tried, Nicole was much too conscious of Slade. His light blue button-up shirt contrasted with his dark complexion and dark hair. If she were honest with herself, she'd have to admit he was the most handsome man she'd seen in a long time.

But she wasn't ready to be honest with herself. Handsome couldn't make up for what his jock friends did to her in high school.

That was a lifetime ago.

So much has happened since then. Why am I still holding a grudge?

The waitress brought over a tray of eggs and pancakes and grits giving her a reprieve from the past. Em's pancakes were in the shape of mouse ears. Em started talking about how these were her favorite pancakes in the whole world and how they should come to this restaurant every day. Nicole laughed at her daughter even though Em said the same thing every time they ate breakfast here. She was happy the conversation could be directed at something besides Slade Larson.

When they were almost finished eating, Nicole caught movement from Slade's side of the room and before she knew it, he was standing at their table.

"Nicole, I didn't want to leave without telling you hello." He looked at Emily and stuck out his hand. "Hello, Emily, you certain look pretty today."

Emily looked at Nicole. "You can shake Mr. Larson's hand, Emily. It's okay."

Emily smiled and stuck out her hand.

"My brother told me to say hello if I saw you again."

"I know Mr. Mac. He's nice. Mama said she and my daddy sang at Mr. Mac's restaurant."

"They certainly did."

"She doesn't sing anymore except at church," Emily said, "but sometimes she sings to me when we're by ourselves."

Slade looked at Nicole then back at Emily. "You're a lucky girl."

"Slade," Nicole said, "I'd like to introduce you to Miss Tillie Mason. She and her husband knew you a long time ago."

Slade's face got serious. Nicole could tell he was trying to place her.

Miss Tillie stuck out her hand. "My husband had Coastal Tours a long time ago when your dad first opened the restaurant. You and Mac were young men still in high school so I'm sure you don't remember me."

"You're right. I don't remember meeting you but I do remember your husband and his great tour busses. He was perfect for the business. Everyone loved him." Miss Tillie looked down at the table for a second, took a deep breath, then smiled. "Thank you for saying that. I thought he was as well."

Slade turned back to Nicole. "I'll be in town a few days helping Mac so you might see me in your café. I loved that shrimp salad." He smiled at Emily. "And I'm so glad I've gotten to see you again, Miss Emily."

Emily giggled.

"Ladies." He nodded, then walked back to his table.

"I like him, Mama. He's nice."

"Yes, he is." *There's no reason to let my child know how I really feel about the man.* "It was nice of him to come over to our table."

By the time they finished breakfast, she realized Slade had left the café, and as she walked outside, she found herself looking around the parking lot. What did he drive? Where was he staying? Was he meeting someone?

"Can we go out on the pier? Look, that boat has stuff he caught last night." Em pulled Nicole's hand and she let her daughter lead the way down the pier.

The warm breeze blew through her hair. She raised her face to the cloudless sky and thought how nice it would be to walk along the pier with a man the way she and Tony used to do before their lives were consumed by their restaurant.

Those were such precious, loving days. As she looked down at Em, she knew today was just as wonderful. When Em was happy and healthy, she was happy.

She held Em's hand as they watched the men scoop up shrimp from big ice chests and weigh them for people standing around wanting to buy fresh seafood. Nicole always loved watching this scene, but what she enjoyed more was the way her daughter enjoyed herself.

She wondered if Slade had stopped to notice what was happening on the pier. Did he care what happened in this part of the coast or was he here to finish with Mac's problems as quickly as possible so he could hurry back to wherever he lived?

"Can we still go to the beach?"

Em's question pulled her out of her reverie about a man she didn't know.

"Yes, of course, we can go for a little while."

She still had time to enjoy Em at the beach. Later today she had a guitar lesson for a young boy. She looked forward to working with the student who was eager to learn what she had to show him. Happy students and satisfied parents spread the word to bring in more students, giving her hope she'd one day have enough money to pay Barry Keats.

That's what she needed to be thinking about, not about a man from someplace else messing with life in Marsh Isles.

Chapter Three

Thoughts of Nicole lingered in his mind as Slade Larson walked out into the lush landscaping of his beachside hotel. He thought about Nicole and her daughter. After finding out she was the lady from whom his company had acquired The Yellow Rooster, he couldn't push her image out of his thoughts.

It wasn't often he let his business decisions become personal. Years ago when he'd left the coast and found his mark in New York, he learned to keep business and his personal life apart, but meeting Nicole touched his heart. Mac filled him in about her life with Tony, their singing career, and their misfortune of trying to open their own restaurant.

Now that he owned most of the stock in The Yellow Rooster, he tried not to mention it to Mac since Slade's Seafood Restaurant wasn't doing well. He couldn't deny The Yellow Rooster had something to do with Mac's falling revenue. Slade kept telling himself when the newness wore off, business for the other local restaurants would increase, but in his heart, he knew it would take more than that. Gary had made The Yellow Rooster into a restaurant that would rival any of those Slade frequented in New York.

And then there was Nicole. He had been impressed with her small café. Its local charm should have been enough to pull in local diners and tourists as well, but he knew The Yellow Rooster was hurting her too.

Failing businesses was a subject Slade dealt with every day. A viable solution was always available even if it meant selling to a company like his own. Acquisitions like those had made him rich. He never lost sleep over buying failing businesses. In fact, he'd convinced himself he did the owners a favor by helping them unload projects they could no longer handle.

But after meeting Nicole and her daughter, he'd tossed and turned in his hotel room all night. Knowing how hard her life must be, it was impossible not to feel something. He couldn't imagine taking care of a child alone, especially a sick child. In fact, he couldn't imagine having the responsibility of a child at all.

He left his beachside hotel and drove north across the bay bridge. The shoreline of Marsh Isles stood out across the water. The Yellow Rooster stood out over the line of new businesses. He was proud of what he and Gary had done.

Too bad Nicole's husband didn't have the same kind of business head that Gary has.

That wasn't his problem, of course. He believed that choices a person made in life had to be dealt with and accepted. If they turned out to be bad choices, a person had to deal with that as well.

That thought made him pause. He, too, had made

choices in life, some good, some bad. Some of those choices made the possibility of having a family slim to none. Work had become his life. He loved his hectic work routine. After several failed relationships, he'd decided to forgo looking for a woman to share his life. Except for the occasional social where he was expected to bring a date, he realized his single status and blossoming company attracted the kind of women he could never love. "Looking for a rich husband" should've been written across their foreheads. They were usually well-dressed and gorgeous, but he didn't need a trophy wife. He'd choose a solitary existence any day and be happy about it.

Instead of going to The Yellow Rooster as he wanted to do, he pulled in front of Slade's and sat a moment. He had a good life. His bank account was brimming over. His businesses were profitable, and he had the respect of his fellow businessmen.

His business plan was working. He wanted for nothing.

"Yeah, right." He slammed the door then he took the few steps to his brother's restaurant, not allowing himself to harbor thoughts that would ruin his happiness.

He expected to see Mac somewhere in the restaurant, but James, the bar-back was stocking the drink cooler.

"Hey, James, where's my brother?"

"Don't know. I opened for him this morning. From the look of the near-empty coolers and the mess around the tables, he must've stayed open late last night."

"Thanks. Had I known he wouldn't be in, I could've gotten here earlier to help you."

"No problem. I'm an early riser."

Slade smiled. He was a morning person as well.

He walked through the restaurant and frowned at the lingering odor of smoke. After the last of the dinner guests left the dining room, music in the attached lounge entertained patrons for as long as they ordered drinks. Smoking was allowed in the lounge, but it never quite cleared away from the restaurant area. Having a non-smoking establishment or installing a better ventilation system was the first thing Slade suggested to Mac. The suggestion didn't go over well.

Now standing at the door of the office, he took in the chaos he'd tried to organize for the last few days. How could anyone let a business get in such a mess?

He let out a loud huff and headed to the desk where he'd made a workspace and hoped he'd find a little profit from last night's late night. He wanted his brother to reap the fruits of his hard work and wished he had a magic solution to his problems.

While he waited for the computer to warm up, he stared at the calendar. His flight home was scheduled for tomorrow morning. He'd been here for almost a week, but he knew he needed much more time here to help Mac. Things were in a bigger mess than he ever imagined.

Maybe it was partly his fault. No, not "partly." He'd been a stranger to Slade's Restaurant since he'd left the area. Had he stayed in Marsh Isles, he could've helped Mac with the business. He was here now, but he knew he'd need more time if something was to be done to put some life back in Slade's Restaurant.

He pulled his cell from his pocket, then hit his personal secretary's number. Hiring Kelli was the best business decision he'd ever made. She kept his life as uncomplicated as it could possibly be.

Fifteen minutes later, Slade hung up knowing his daily updates and his weekly schedule. With a few cancellations and several reschedules, Kelli straightened out his next two weeks so he could stay on the coast a little longer. He had three important phone calls and one conference call he could do from here. Satisfied what he was doing was the right decision, he tackled the books from the restaurant once more and hoped for a miracle.

For the next thirty minutes he went through folder after folder and piles of receipts and tried to do a spreadsheet that would help Mac understand what he was doing and where his problems might be.

Right before nine he heard James and Mac talking. He leaned back in his chair and waited for his brother to come in. He knew Mac worked late hours, but there was so much he and Mac needed to do he had hoped his brother would've come in early to help get the mess organized.

"Hey, brother, you're here early," Mac said as he strolled into the office.

Only thirteen months separated Mac and him, but Slade always felt Mac was the mature, much older brother. He was slightly bigger than Slade and had been a football star in his own right and had played on the college level. Slade always looked up to him and was as devastated as he was when Mac hurt his shoulder and had to drop out of sports.

Today Mac seemed as big as ever. His stature and personality seemed to suck the air out of a room when he walked in. Tall, with broad shoulders, and a fit body,

Slade could tell he still tried to take care of himself. As handsome as ever with the Larson traits of dark hair and dark brown eyes, Mac had aged nicely.

"Not really early," Slade said. "I wanted to get some work done before we opened for business. I just assumed you'd be here."

"Yeah," Mac said as he plopped down in an old chair that had been their dad's. "I would've been here to help, but I had to get some sleep or I wouldn't be able to be here at all. We closed the kitchen the usual time, but there was a party of twelve that sat around until one-thirty this morning. I kept them supplied with small dishes and they were happy to have a place to socialize. Tucker Ladnier, my singer, stayed until almost midnight. Sunday isn't always a good night for us, so I wasn't about to run off a group of paying customers."

"I understand. I just went through the receipts and I can report you made a profit last night. I didn't mean to sound like I don't empathize with the type of job you have and the hours you keep."

Mac stretched out his legs. "You could've fooled me. I have a feeling you think I'm playing around all day and all night and letting this place go to the dogs."

"No, Mac. I know you're not playing . . ."

Mac cut him off. "Yeah, well, you have a heck of a way of showing it. You come down here from your big city office and start finding fault with the way I'm running this place. If you cared anything about the lounge, you'd be here helping instead of living the high life in New York."

Slade stared at his brother before he said something they'd both regret. Mac was tired and overworked.

Finally, he leaned back in the desk chair. "You're right. I do live in a big city. I don't work your late hours nor do I have to deal with a bunch of unruly tourists, but I chose to leave that type of work after seeing what it did to our family. You do remember what it did to our family, right? From the earliest time I can remember, Mom and Dad fought and it was always over something to do with this place and the hours Dad stayed away from his family."

Mac stood up. His brows were drawn. "Don't start that. You couldn't cut it here. You needed a softer, plusher life than running a restaurant and lounge. You even have someone else running that Yellow Chicken of yours."

"It's The Yellow Rooster." He corrected his brother with a light tone, knowing Mac was trying to make fun of the name. He wasn't going to get into an argument this morning. "Mac, when I left here I wasn't looking for an easier life. I wanted one that gave me a little more satisfaction."

"And more money."

"Yes, and more money. Our dad worked his fingers to the bone and when he died, he had nothing but debts." Slade pulled in his temper. "I'll tell you right now from the looks of these books, you're going to be in his same shape."

Mac walked to the window, but Slade knew he couldn't see anything through the dirty film that covered it.

"Mac, I don't want you to think I don't understand how hard you work here. It's not an easy life." Slade chuckled. "Maybe I *was* looking for something easier when I left, but I have to tell you that doing what I do isn't always a bed of roses. It's a different kind of work and a different kind of stress, but it's definitely there."

Mac turned around. "I love this place. It's my life, and I give it all I have."

Slade stepped toward him and placed a hand on his shoulder. "I know you do, but sometimes we need help doing even the things we love."

Mac nodded. "You're right. I'm not blind, but I don't know where to start. We've run this business the same way since Dad opened it."

"Maybe that's the problem." He gave his brother a slight nudge on the arm. "We'll figure it out."

Slade walked back to his desk and sat down. "I went to The Yellow Rooster yesterday and talked to Gary."

Mac grumbled something.

"The Yellow Rooster is on fire right now, but I can't take credit for it. It's new and it's one of the up-and-coming places on the coast, and I wanted to see what Gary was doing."

"And?"

"And what I saw impressed the heck out of me. Gary has made that place top notch. The menu is trendy, but has enough local cuisine to satisfy everyone. I even went over to Tony's Place and met Nicole Russo. Even though her café isn't doing as well as Gary's, she has some nice touches. I ordered the shrimp salad and I have to say, it's the best I've ever had."

Mac's eyebrows came together. "So, did Nicole remember you?"

"Unfortunately, she remembered me from high school, but I didn't remember her."

"I can see why you didn't. She was several years

behind me, but I do remember her as being really shy. She kind of melted into the walls."

"She doesn't anymore. She's really very attractive and from what I saw, isn't shy anymore. She made it clear she remembered me as being one of 'those jocks' as she called us."

"Ouch. That must've hurt your ego."

"Yes, it did. I'm not sure why she has it in for me and my friends. We didn't do her anything."

Mac raised his eyebrow.

"What?"

"You don't remember, do you?"

"Give me a hint here. I have no idea what you're talking about."

"Some of your football friends thought it would be funny to send her secret admirer letters. I was out of school by then, but I even heard about it."

Slade thought a minute, then grimaced. "That was her? No wonder she thinks all jocks are crude and unfeeling." Slade looked up at Mac. "But I had no part in that. Do you think I'm some kind of monster with no feelings?"

"No, but if you knew they were doing it, you could've stopped them."

Slade squeezed his eyes. "You're right. I could've stepped in and stopped them or warned her what they were doing." Slade dropped his head. "Maybe I am a monster."

Mac cracked a smile. "No, you weren't a monster, just a stupid jock back then."

"I like to think I've outgrown those stupid characteristics." He cleared his throat. "Let's get to work and see if we can make some sense of this mess before customers start coming in."

Mac was right. He was never an unfeeling monster, but he was afraid Nicole would think he was if she ever found out he hadn't told her right away it was his company that had bought her husband's restaurant.

~

Nicole wiped the table after the last of her dinner customers left. She'd had a decent night, but had hoped for more customers. She'd tried something different by spending extra money on a folding sign to go outside on the sidewalk. Tonight the sign featured broiled snapper. Those who ordered it raved about it, but the numbers who walked through the door were not enough.

She walked to the window and frowned. Customers still filed into The Yellow Rooster as they had been doing all night.

When she was satisfied that the dining area looked neat, she stuck her head in the kitchen. "Clark, I'm walking across to see what our competition is doing tonight."

"Yeah, I've been seeing the cars out my window. They sure know how to draw the crowds."

"Do you blame the tourists? That gorgeous sign and yellow building puts mine to shame."

"Your building is neat and clean."

"Neat and clean, but not exciting and new, but thanks for trying to make me feel good."

Clark chuckled. "I'll call you if I need you. Go enjoy the music over there."

Clark Evans had started a little over a week ago and was doing a great job. She walked out the front door with a smile on her face that quickly turned into a frown when she saw a city tractor working alongside on the street not far from her building. "Always something," she said. "No wonder more people didn't come in tonight."

She walked over to the workmen and found out they were fixing a leak in the water main and would be finished shortly, but the workman told her the telephone line to her restaurant had been cut. "I was getting ready to come talk with you. We have someone from the telephone company on his way. I'm sure it'll be fixed shortly."

Thanking them, she headed across the street and into The Yellow Rooster.

Most of tables were still full even though it was almost nine o'clock, so she chose a stool at the counter. Immediately a young man handed her a glass of water and a menu. She studied the menu carefully. Gary's selection was longer than hers, but not so spectacular that they'd draw the crowds.

Looking around, she knew the draw was the building, the décor and the fabulous musicians. She could compete with the food, but not with the rest.

She glanced at the stage and listened closely to the singer. His voice sounded phenomenal. She knew the equipment helped with the sound, but it didn't matter. His music selection was great and the diners loved him.

On days like today she missed Tony the most. This should've been his restaurant. This should've been their stage. Their spotlight. Their accolades.

But, of course, it wasn't. She'd convinced herself a long time ago she was content with being a café owner, but she wondered if she'd ever have the nerve to sing again in a venue like this. The stage now belonged to others, not her. She looked at the singer with longing, then shook her head and made her selection on the menu.

As she waited for her food, she made herself comfortable listening to the soothing music. The waiter told her the singer's name was Tucker Ladnier.

"Thank you. I think I've heard him at Slade's."

The singer's mellow voice floated throughout the dining area, reminding Nicole of Tony's rich voice. She closed her eyes and let his melody soothe her. Maybe one day she could afford to have entertainment for her customers as well. When his song ended, she clapped along with everyone in the dining area.

Shortly after her food was served, someone walked up behind her stool.

She turned to find Slade Larson. "Slade, what are you doing here? Does Mac know you're checking up on the competition?"

His face was serious. His brows knitted. He reached out and took her hand. She could tell something was wrong.

As a mother with a child who wasn't in the best of health, her first thought was of Emily. "Slade, what's wrong?"

"Mac asked me to come get you. Your cook told me you were here."

"What? I have no idea what you're talking about."

"It's your daughter. Mac couldn't leave the restaurant and wanted me to take you to the hospital." He grabbed her hand and squeezed. "She's okay. Miss Tillie called an ambulance."

Nicole didn't ask anything else. Together she and Slade ran out the door.

"My car is right here." He pulled open the door.

"I'll get you to the hospital."

Nicole slid into the car not able to think about anything but Emily. What had happened? Had she passed out again? Gotten sick? Or maybe she'd had an accident at school today.

Her thoughts scattered.

When Slade opened his door and jumped into the car, she realized she had no idea how this man knew what was happening and she didn't.

He pulled his seatbelt across his body, gave her a quick look, then pulled away from the curb. "We'll be there in a matter of minutes."

"What happened? Why wasn't I called?" Her words barely were audible.

"I'm not sure. Miss Tillie couldn't get you on your phone or the café phone. She had Mac's number at the restaurant and knew he'd help. The only thing he told me was that one of us needed to get you to the hospital."

"Thank you." Again, her words didn't sound like her own voice.

She found her phone in her purse, realized she had turned off the ringer, then read the short text message from Miss Tillie. Quickly she hit her number. No one answered. If the lady was with Emily in the emergency room, she would've turned her phone off. She wrote a quick text. "I figured she wouldn't be able to answer, but I had to try."

Nicole glanced over at Slade. He nodded.

How could he look so cool and collected? The nighttime traffic was unexpectedly awful going across the bay bridge. Bumper to bumper. Hardly moving, but Slade wasn't rattled. Finally he turned onto the off ramp, but came to a complete stop.

He mumbled something under his breath and hit the steering wheel with his hand. At least he was human. She looked at the cars in front of theirs.

Please. Please. Move. Emily needs me. She'll be scared.

She squeezed her eyes and tried to breath normally.

"You okay?" Slade's words got her attention.

She looked directly into his eyes. "No."

He nodded. "I understand. Well, not really. I don't have children. I can't imagine how you must feel." He reached across the seat and touched her hand. "We'll be there as soon as these cars move. Emily's okay."

Nicole looked down at his hand, pushed down a knot in her throat and nodded. "I hope so. Did someone say what happened?"

Slowly he pulled his hand away. "No. Mac was panicky and said to go. He didn't tell me what happened."

He spoke, but she didn't follow his words. He had touched her hand. This stranger. This man who had once made her feel insignificant in high school didn't feel like a stranger or a bad human being at the moment. He'd offered her understanding and strength. A man had not held her hand or held her since Tony had died. Slade's contact was brief, but it was as though he had pulled her into his arms and hugged her tightly offering her what she needed. And, she did need his support. At the moment, anyone's support.

She pushed that thought aside. Right now Emily needed her and she would find the strength to stand by her child as she'd always done. It didn't matter that a man's shoulder, or touch, or hug would make her life easier. She could do this with or without it.

"Great," he said under his breath. "Cars are moving."

She looked at him as if for the first time. Here in the car, just inches from her, she saw his features clearly. The straight nose, the dark eyes, and dark brows to match his slightly wavy black hair made him the classic dark and handsome male, especially with the almost constant five o'clock shadow.

Tony had been dark complexioned with black hair and dark eyes also, but he was shorter and more muscular. He was nice looking in his own way, but Slade was absolutely gorgeous.

Feeling guilty that she'd compared Tony's and Slade's looks, she put her head down. *Oh, Tony. I need you.*

She let out a long breath, closed her eyes and prayed to have the strength to do what needed to be done for Emily.

As soon as Slade pulled in front of the hospital Emergency wing, she got out. "Thank you," she managed to say as she spun around and ran into the building. Unfortunately, she knew her way around this hospital. Between Tony and Emily, she had been in and out of here more times than she cared to count.

Now what mattered was finding her daughter.

"My daughter's here. Emily Russo," she told the nurse behind the window. "Please. I need to go to her."

"Of course, Mrs. Russo."

Nicole waited as patiently as possible as the nurse made a call. Almost immediately, the double doors opened and a male nurse stepped out.

"Mrs. Russo? We have Emily in the back. You can

follow me."

Nicole followed close behind the man in green scrubs, all the time praying that her daughter was okay. The paintings on the wall and the shiny tiles on the floor were all a blur as she followed the young man down one hall and then another where he stopped and held the door open for her.

"I'll have one of the doctors come in to explain what's happening."

Miss Tillie sat in a chair on the side of the bed holding Emily's hand. Miss Tillie looked up and smiled at Nicole. "She's going to be okay."

Emily opened her eyes and smiled. "Mommy. You came."

"Of course, I came," Nicole said as she walked up to the bed, bent over and hugged her daughter. She held her tightly with the child's head tucked in her neck. "Oh, Baby. I'm so sorry I didn't get here quicker. I was at work. Mr. Slade came to get me and we got here as fast as we could."

"Is Mr. Slade here with you?"

"No, he had to get back to work."

"Miss Tillie told me she called you. She got to ride in the ambulance with me."

Nicole looked over at Miss Tillie, reached out and took her hand. "I can't thank you enough."

"That's not necessary. I was told the phone at the restaurant was down and you didn't answer your cell."

"I'm sorry. I had my ringer off, and workman fixing a leaking pipe outside the restaurant cut the telephone line. Thanks for calling Mac. What happened?"

"I was running her bath water and she simply slipped to the floor and nearly passed out. Got real white and sweaty."

Nicole looked up at the unit of blood they were giving to Emily. "Did they say if she'd need more than this one?"

"They're hoping this one will do the job."

"Me too," Nicole whispered. She held her daughter's hand and silently said a prayer of thanks for whoever had donated the blood that once again was saving her daughter.

Chapter Four

Slade watched Nicole run through the doors of the Emergency Room before he pulled into a parking space. He sat for a few minutes with his hands on the wheel. He knew he should get back to the restaurant to help Mac, but he couldn't make himself leave Nicole. Miss Tillie would probably need a ride home so he used that as an excuse to go inside.

He knew giving Miss Tillie a ride wasn't the real reason he was staying, but it would have to do.

Stepping out of the car, the warmth from the parking lot concrete closed in around him even though the sun had set hours ago. In a way it reminded him of the hot sidewalks in New York in the middle of summer, but in the city he was able to avoid the heat by staying in his air conditioned office. This was almost the end of August and the heat was brutal.

Might as well embrace it while I'm here. It'll be snowing in New York before I know it.

As he walked toward the entrance of the hospital, he

remembered being in this same hospital during the hot summer when he was about ten. He'd fallen off his bicycle and broken a collarbone. He remembered the hard, hot asphalt he'd fallen on as if it were yesterday. It wasn't often he reminisced about his childhood here on the coast because every time he did, visions of his parents arguing and screaming at each other took over. There were very few good memories of his family being together.

The only other time he'd been here was when his dad died. He'd come with Mac to see the body before it was taken to the morgue. He'd been so young. He had just graduated from college and wanted to move someplace else, but he stayed to help Mac keep their dad's business open.

So much had happened since Slade's Seafood Restaurant had been dumped into his and Mac's laps.

He was a different man now. Maybe before he left the coast, he'd take a ride through the neighborhood where he and Mac had grown up and visit the beach where they'd played. Maybe Nicole would come along. He'd love to show her a part of his past life.

That thought nearly floored him. Did he really want to form an attachment to Nicole and to Em? He'd thought about asking her out to get a cup of coffee after work. It didn't have to mean anything, but sharing your past did mean something.

He entered the cool air of the Emergency Room. He wasn't even sure he'd be allowed to get in to see Nicole, but he knew he couldn't leave without trying. He wasn't sure why it meant so much to him, but it did.

The nurse at the ER station was accommodating, even walking with him toward Emily's small room.

"We normally allow only two visitors per unit," she said as they walked down an immaculate hall, "but we're not very busy tonight."

"Thank you. I appreciate your doing this. I don't plan to stay very long. I think one of the ladies might need a ride home."

With a sweet smile, the nurse left him. Slade tapped on the door and opened it slightly. Nicole sat on the side of the bed talking to Miss Tillie.

"Is it okay to come in?"

"Slade? I can't believe you're still here." Nicole's face softened with a smile.

"I wanted to check on Emily before I left." He stepped near the bed and was shocked to see the child was receiving blood. "Has she been awake?"

"On and off. She's just really tired."

Slade watched Nicole closely as she spoke softly and calmly about her little girl. He wasn't sure what was wrong with the child's health but it couldn't be good if she was getting blood. His heart went out to the mother of this child, and at the same time felt a sharp band of regret, or maybe it was guilt, for adding to her sorrows by buying her husband's lounge for such a low price.

"Slade, you remember Miss Tillie from breakfast? She's been my life-saver since we moved here, and today was no different."

"How do you do, Mr. Larson?"

"I'm fine now that I see little Em is doing okay." He looked at Nicole and cleared his throat. "Will she be able to go home tonight?"

With a smile, Nicole nodded. "We think so. The doctor came in and said she'd only need this one unit today. We're waiting for some test results before he lets her go."

Slade glanced up at the IV bag, then at the child on the bed, her black hair spread out over the pillow. She was a beautiful little girl. He took a deep breath, then spoke to Miss Tillie. "Ma'am, if you're ready to go home, I can take you home, then if Emily is discharged, I can run back over here and give them a ride home."

"Oh no," Nicole said. "I couldn't ask you to do that?"

"Nicole, it's no problem, and if you remember, your vehicle is at your restaurant. I'll come back, but you can call me if she's ready to leave before I get here." He pulled a card from his wallet, realized it had his investment company's name on it and decided not to give it to Nicole. She probably remembered the name of the company who bought her restaurant.

Instead of the card, he wrote his cell number on a piece of paper. "I insist you call me."

Nicole looked down at his number, then up at him. "You're being way too nice to me."

Slade chuckled. "Not really. I can't see you taking your daughter home in one of those pink taxis."

That brought a smile to her face.

"Now, that's better. Your smiles are way too beautiful to hide."

Miss Tillie stood up, walked around the bed and pulled Nicole into her arms. "I'll fix you a little something to eat. I'm sure you haven't had a thing since breakfast."

Nicole stepped away. "What would I do without you?"

"No, dear. You do more for this old lady than you'll

ever know." She bent down and kissed Emily on the forehead, took a ragged breath, then picked up her purse. "Young man, I'm ready if you are."

Slade looked back at Nicole before stepping out of the room. "Don't you dare call a taxi." He winked at her and left.

~

Nicole watched Slade disappear into the hallway. For the first time since he'd rushed into The Yellow Rooster, she took a calming breath and relaxed against the straight-backed chair. How could this be the same obnoxious man she knew from high school?

"Mama?"

Nicole sat up straight. "I'm right here, Em."

"Where's Miss Tillie?"

"She went home."

"With Mr. Mac's brother?"

"You saw him? I thought you were asleep."

"I was but I woke up and peeked. I like him. He's nice."

Nicole didn't answer, but she had to admit Slade Larson had a side to him that appealed to her. She smiled down at her daughter. "I think he likes you too."

Emily looked at the IV in her arm, closed her eyes and slipped back off to sleep.

For a girl of six, she shouldn't know what a transfusion was, but this little girl did. How many had she had in her short life?

How many more would she need before something more could to be done to save her life?

~

Several hours later Slade stepped softly through the door to Emily's room, but immediately stopped. Emily was asleep with the covers pulled up to her chin. Nicole still sat in the chair but was bent over with her head on the bed. She too looked to be asleep.

What a beautiful sight.

Her long blond hair, falling down across her face, was streaked with highlights in just the right places. Slade had a feeling those streaks weren't from some expensive salon. The Gulf Coast sun would've put them there naturally. He liked that.

He had never thought about having kids and had never been close to anyone with kids except for Mac whose two daughters lived with their mother on the West Coast. Slade knew his career and lifestyle kept him from forming any serious relationships with the women he infrequently took out. His solitary existence wasn't something he thought about often, but at times like this, loneliness crashed down on him like a ton of bricks.

He shook his head and consciously pushed those emotions aside.

The door squeaked. Nicole sat up and looked at him.

"Slade. You're back."

"Yep. I said I would be. I ran by the restaurant, gave Mac a hand for a short time, but he had things under control. He was more concerned about Emily and you, and he nearly pushed me out the door to get back up here."

Nicole smiled big. "Mac's been a good friend to me."

"He thinks the world of you and Em. Have they said when she can leave?"

"Shortly. They removed the IV about thirty minutes

ago. We're waiting on the discharge papers. It shouldn't be much longer."

Slade pulled a chair up to the bed. "So I assume the IV did its job."

Nicole looked at Emily, then back at him, the smile gone from her face. "For the time being."

"Miss Tillie said you end up here quite a bit. Is there nothing more they can do to keep this from happening?"

Nicole looked down then swallowed. "Right now transfusions work, but she can't do this the rest of her life."

He hesitated with his next question, but he had to know. "This is the same disease that your husband had?"

"Yes."

For a moment Slade thought she wouldn't say any more, but then looked up at him.

"It's a blood disease. Tony didn't show signs until he was in his thirties. He downplayed his fatigue and, well, I now know he flat-out lied to me. He never told me what he had, but obviously it was serious. Every once in a while he saw a doctor, but it never occurred to me that something was wrong. I always assumed he was having regular checkups. Who knew I was so wrong and oblivious?" Nicole took a deep breath. "I have a feeling his lifestyle at the lounges didn't help the situation. Looking back I can see he didn't take care of himself. Maybe had he listened to a doctor, he'd be with us today."

"I'm sorry, Nicole. I know it's none of my business."

"No, you're wrong. You're here and you've helped

me. I consider that a reason for you to understand what's happening to my Em." She glanced at the child before continuing. "Children sometimes inherit the disease early in life. I guess Em was one of the unlucky ones." She went on to explain a little about the disease, speaking in soft tones so as not to wake her daughter.

Slade leaned back against the chair, his mind taking in all that Nicole was saying. She picked her words carefully, explaining what might have to be done in the future, but she never used the words "life-threatening" even though Slade knew it could be since the disease took her husband's life. Miss Tillie had told him enough on her ride home to make him understand the situation would one day be dire.

Then she shocked him. "Tony kept his illness a secret until the very end when he had to be admitted to the hospital. At that point, there was nothing anyone could do for him. After his death, when Em started showing signs, I realized he harmed more than himself by keeping his secret. Had we known maybe we could've done something earlier." Her words were almost a whisper, but Slade heard. She looked up. "I'm sorry. I shouldn't have said that."

"It's okay, Nicole. The well-being of your child is foremost and, of course, you'd think that."

He wanted to ask if she had taken her to a specialist, but the door opened and a nurse walked in carrying a stack of papers. Slade sat quietly as Nicole signed papers and listened to the routine discharge orders.

"Is she dressed and ready to go?" the nurse asked.

"Yes." Nicole leaned over the bed. "Em, wake up, sweetie. It's time to go home."

Emily opened her eyes, but didn't say anything.

The nurse and Nicole helped her out of bed and into the wheelchair. When she saw Slade, she smiled.

"Hey, Mr. Slade." Her words were barely audible, but her smile said it all.

"Hey, Miss Em. Ready to go home?"

Slade's heart broke watching a girl so young go through so much. He wished there was something he could do to help, but knowing Nicole was so self-sufficient, he had a feeling his help wasn't something she'd allow.

He'd have to work on changing her mind.

As soon as that thought materialized he knew getting involved with Nicole and Emily was not part of his plan for being in Marsh Isles.

But could he just walk away?

Neither he nor Nicole talked much on the way home. Nicole sat in the back seat and held her daughter's hand. Emily spoke a little but Slade couldn't hear what she was saying. By the time he pulled in front of Nicole's house, he'd made up his mind to make a few calls to some of his acquaintances in New York who had connections in the medical field. He knew nothing about the disease Em had, but it was not below him to ask for help from someone who did.

Nicole helped Emily out of the car, but the little girl wobbled. Slade took two big steps and scooped her into his arms. The smile he received warmed his heart again.

"Thanks, Mr. Mac." She put her arms around his neck and snuggled up next to his neck.

"No problem, but call me Mr. Slade. Mr. Mac is my brother."

"I forgot."

"That's okay. We all forget things. I know I forget a

lot." He stepped through the door Nicole held open for him, relishing the feel of the little girl holding onto him. What would it be like to have a child of your own, to protect a child, and to love a child? Those thoughts collided within him as he carried her into the house. "Where do you want her?"

"I want to go to my room," Emily said before Nicole could answer.

Slade looked at Nicole.

"I guess her room is where we'll take her," Nicole said.

Slade glanced around at the neat little house as he passed through the living room and into a short hallway, then followed Nicole into a room that was definitely a little girl's room. He couldn't remember ever being in a room quite like this with its lavender and pink décor from the floor to the ceiling.

"On the bed?" he asked.

"Yes, sir." Emily's answer was soft, almost a whisper.

Nicole pulled back the lavender spread decorated in what looked like fairy princesses, but he couldn't be sure. Gently he laid her on pink sheets.

"Thanks, Mr. Slade."

"You are most welcome, Little Princess."

Emily pulled the blanket up to her eyes and laughed.

Nicole turned on the TV then adjusted the blanket. "Mr. Slade and I will be in the kitchen. Miss Tillie put a pot of your favorite soup on the stove. Can I fix you a bowl?"

"Ice cream. I'd rather ice cream. Chocolate."

"Ice cream?" Nicole laughed. "Okay. I'll bring it

in."

Slade followed Nicole out of Emily's room, feeling awkward and definitely out of place in this little girl's world, but as he stepped into the small kitchen he felt better. Stainless appliances and a modern granite countertop made him a more comfortable.

Nicole fixed a bowl of ice cream, then took it to Emily.

When she got back in the kitchen, she went to the sink, placed her hands on the countertop and seemed to slump.

Slade hesitated. He didn't know this lady very well, but when her body seemed to quiver, he stepped next to her and put his arm around her shoulders. "It's okay not to be strong all the time."

Her shoulders shook beneath his hands. He turned her and she collapsed into his arms. With her head against his chest and her hands grabbing a bunch of his shirt, she sobbed.

Slade held her tightly and let her cry. He placed his chin in her hair, held her against his body and had the strongest urge to never let her go, to protect her against the uncertain world she faced with her daughter. He closed his eyes. Even with the same clothes she had on from her café, she smelled sweet and fresh.

She trembled.

He pulled her closer.

When was the last time he'd held a female against him? Holding Nicole felt natural and right.

Finally, with a shudder, she stepped away. He kept his hands on her shoulders as she got control of her jagged breaths.

"I'm so sorry. I try not to do that. It doesn't help the

situation."

He held her at arm's length. "Don't ever apologize for showing your emotions. Your daughter is sick. She needs you, but you need someone once in a while to give you a little support. I'm glad I happened to be here with an empty shoulder."

She sniffled, smiled, then looked up. Her blue eyes were red and swollen.

She was beautiful.

"Thank you. I guess I needed to let a little of those sobs out." She ran her hand across his shirt where she'd held on for dear life. "I'm so sorry. If you want, I can throw it in the dryer to get the wrinkles out."

"Absolutely not. I'm sure no one at Slade's is going to notice a few wrinkles."

She looked around the kitchen and inhaled deeply. "I could use a bowl of Miss Tillie's soup. Would you like a bowl with me? Or I could fix you a bowl of ice cream." She smiled.

"I'll take you up on some soup. I haven't had homemade soup in years."

He watched her move mechanically as she lit the gas range under the pot, then took two bowls and two glasses down from the cabinet. When she opened the drawer for the silverware, Slade stepped next to her and grabbed two spoons.

She smiled. "Thanks. Except for Miss Tillie, I'm not used to having anyone in the kitchen."

"I'll sit down out of the way if you'd like."

"No, not at all," she said as she put the bowls on two bright yellow placemats, then pulled out two cloth napkins and put them near the bowls.

"Paper napkins are fine. You don't have to make

more work for yourself."

"No, Em and I use cloth napkins at most of our meals. I know it's silly, but we don't have much anymore but we don't have to wallow in our bad luck. We both like pretty things and I see no reason to not indulge in the simple things we can afford."

"That's a good philosophy." Slade looked around, all of a sudden feeling awkward with the lavish lifestyle he was fortunate enough to have when this beautiful lady was content and happy with the simple things in life for herself and her daughter. "While you finish getting the soup ready, would it be okay if I go check on Em?"

"Please. She'd like that."

Slade headed toward the girly domain and hoped Emily wouldn't kick him out, but he had to step away from Nicole. The cloth napkins and her way of making hers and Emily's lives richer had become so foreign to him since he'd made his fortune in the business world. His life consisted of formal meetings, formal gatherings, and restaurants with white tablecloths. He'd never look at a cloth napkin again without thinking about Nicole and her daughter.

He tapped lightly on Em's door. She didn't answer. He cracked the door and peeked in. She was asleep, the empty ice cream bowl by her pillow. He walked over to the bed, picked up the remote and turned off the TV, then took the bowl away. Even though he'd never tucked a child in before, he pulled the cover up to her chin.

With the dirty bowl in his hand, he stood at the bedside and looked at the child. So sweet. So innocent yet knowing way too much about hospitals and doctors.

He swallowed. There had to be something he could do to help.

~

Nicole looked up when Slade stepped into the kitchen.

"She was already asleep, but she'd eaten all her ice cream." He showed her the empty bowl then placed it in the sink.

"Good. I should've been in there with her instead of leaning against you crying." She wiped her hand across her face as if she were brushing away her embarrassment of crying on his shoulder. "I never let her see me upset over her health. I felt it coming and had to get out of there."

"That little girl is wise beyond her years. Even if she saw you cry, I think she'd understand the tears were coming from your love, but she was fine. I'm sure she didn't even realize you weren't there."

"Probably, but we didn't even say our prayers before she fell asleep. I hate it when I'm at work and I know Miss Tillie is tucking her in and saying her prayers with her." With a loud breath, Nicole turned around and placed two bowls of potato soup on the table along with a small bowl of grated cheese, then put a small plate of crackers near them. "I didn't have any bread to put in the oven."

"Crackers are just fine."

Slade pulled out a chair for her. She looked up and blinked, then sat down. He sat across from her.

"This smells delicious."

"Miss Tillie makes sure we're fed properly on the afternoons and evenings I'm at work. I tell her I have time to cook before I leave in the morning, but she insists. She says it gives her something to do so I let her. If I have leftovers at the end of the day, I make sure to call her so we don't have too much food."

"From the way she talks about you two, I'm sure she loves doing it for you ladies."

He picked up a spoon, sprinkled the cheese on the soup, then tasted. "Yep, delicious."

She smiled and did the same. "I'll save some for Emily tomorrow. It's her favorite."

An awkward silence ensued. Finally, Nicole put her spoon down. "I can't thank you enough for all you did today."

"As I said before, you don't have to thank me. I had the time and I made my brother happy in the process."

"I'm still appreciative. I do need to ask you one more favor."

"Sure. I'm at your service," he said with a smile on his face that made her forget he was the troll whom she remembered from high school.

She looked down and picked up her spoon again. "If I can get Miss Tillie to stay with Emily for a few minutes, I need a ride to pick up my car."

"That's simple enough. As soon as we finish this wonderful soup, we can go get your car." Slade scooped up the last of the soup in his bowl. "But first, is there enough soup for me to have another few bites? I'll make sure I leave enough for Emily tomorrow."

"Sure, Miss Tillie always sends over way too much."

He got up, served himself then dove into his second bowl. He was nothing more than a man enjoying a meal, but to Nicole it was the best thing she'd experienced in days even with the fact that he was sitting where Tony always sat.

That thought took her by surprise, but she pushed it aside. There was nothing going on here but feeding a man who had done her a favor.

Nothing else.

So it was okay for him to sit in Tony's chair. Nicole finished her soup and sat quietly as Slade finished his second bowl.

"I'll have to personally thank Miss Tillie for that. I thoroughly enjoyed it," He laughed, "but I guess you could tell that by the way I devoured it." Slade got up and picked up his bowl. "Do you put these in the dishwasher?"

"Today we can. With just the two of us, I usually wash our dishes."

"Then we'll wash." He didn't wait for her to get up, but walked straight to the sink and started running the water.

"Slade, please, just leave them. It'll give me something to do when I get home. I have to stay busy or I think too much."

Slade turned around just enough to look at her. His dark eyes seemed to see right through her. "Staying busy is good. I'm sure you have a lot more to think about than the average mother."

"With Tony gone and Em sick all the time, I can't seem to catch a break." She stopped suddenly. "Sorry again. I swear I'm not a gloomy person. I don't go there often. These last few weeks haven't been good ones."

Slade frowned. "And I'm sure running a restaurant alone is hard on you."

"It is, but it's what all business owners have to face. I really do love having the restaurant. The only part I don't like is being away from Em. I'm not sure what I'd do if Miss Tillie wasn't here to help me."

"Mac said you don't have family here."

"That's right." Nicole explained about how she ended up with the house here. "I'm thankful for what Mom did, and I try to be upbeat for Em and for my customers, but once in a while life seems to get the best."

"You're human, Nicole. And caring. And a loving mother. You'd be inhuman if you didn't worry about your daughter and the life you're giving her."

"You might be right, but I don't like the gloomy Nicole." She pulled in a calming breath and scooted next to him with her dirty dish. What she wanted to do was to throw herself in his arms again. It would feel so good to let someone take the load off her shoulders. But she didn't. Instead she dipped her bowl in the hot soapy water Slade had run and reminded herself Slade Larson was someone who wasn't standing in her kitchen to take any load off her shoulders.

He just happened to be the one Mac had sent to help her.

"Come on. Let's get these dishes done." Slade dipped his hands in the water. "In fact, let me do them and you call Miss Tillie. If she can't come over, I'll run by the lounge and find someone to get your car back to you."

"You're much too nice. If I can figure out where I put my phone, I'll give her a call."

She walked out of the kitchen leaving this stranger at the sink doing her dirty dishes, a stranger who had been her lifesaver today.

Nothing about this situation was right.

She'd figure out a way to solve her problems without Slade, but not before she got her Jeep.

Chapter Five

The next morning, Slade passed by Nicole's café and was surprised to see a "closed" sign still hanging on the door. A light shone through the window so he found a parking place and walked up to the door. After a couple of knocks, a middle aged guy opened the door.

"Sorry but we're closed."

"Yes, I saw the sign, but I was wondering if Ms. Russo's daughter is okay?"

The man thought a moment probably wondering whether to divulge any personal information.

Slade spoke up. "I'm a friend. I was with her at the hospital last night."

The man nodded. "She called to say she was afraid to leave Em with anyone today. I was putting away some things so we wouldn't lose any food."

Slade's mind started spinning. Knowing Nicole was having a hard time, he knew a day closed wasn't going to help her bottom line. He had an idea and hoped it wouldn't make an enemy out of her.

He stepped in and stuck out his hand. He introduced himself. "I don't want to overstep any lines, but my brother and I own Slade's Seafood Restaurant a couple blocks away from here." He purposely left out the part that he also owned Nicole's competition The Yellow Rooster.

"I know exactly where Slade's Restaurant is."

"My brother Mac actually runs the place now, but I'd worked there for years before I moved." Slade hoped his idea he was about to share with this guy wasn't going to make him look like a fool. He took a deep breath.

"I'm well aware of how a restaurant works. I was thinking maybe you and I could open today while Nicole is gone so she doesn't lose any business. If you can handle the kitchen, I'll work the front and maybe we can bring in a few customers and a few dollars. I hate to see her close."

The guy shuffled his feet. "I'm not so sure she'd let us do that. She doesn't ask for much help."

"Yes, I'm well aware of what she'll probably say, but again, I'd hate for her to not open. Do you think you could work the kitchen alone for a few hours? We can do the lunch hour and we'll decide at that point whether to stay open for the dinner meal. I swear. I'll take all the responsibility for this. I'll even call Nicole a little later after we're too far into the day to stop."

This time the guy stuck out his hand to Slade. "I'm Clark Evans. I haven't been here long, but I can whip up most of what she has on the menu. We can't offer her normal daily special, but salads and sandwiches might make her a few dollars today. I'll look in the cooler and see if I can pull a few other things together. I like Nicole. She's the best boss I've ever had. I'd like to lend her a hand."

"Great. I have to call my brother to let him know I won't be in today and then we can look over the menu to see what we can handle."

"A lot of her regulars know Em has a medical condition. They'll understand."

Slade shook his hand again. "It'll be nice working with you."

After deciding which items on the menu Clark could handle alone, Slade asked him to count the money in the register. When Slade felt confident that Nicole wouldn't accuse him of trying to take money from her, he set out getting the front of the restaurant ready for the lunch crowd, and hoped they'd come in.

He glanced over at The Yellow Rooster and wished he could ask Gary to close for today to help out Nicole, but he knew that was ridiculous. He'd opened a fine place to dine, and he wouldn't have it any other way, but for a long, agonizing moment, he felt guilty about owning the restaurant that was taking business away from Nicole.

He wished he'd stuck to his original plan and flipped the building as soon as he'd bought it, but he knew it was too late to think about that now. Knowing he couldn't do anything about The Yellow Rooster and its draw of customers, he turned his attention to Nicole's café.

He had just finished making sure he knew how all of the gadgets worked behind the counter when the first customers walked in. Slade introduced himself and explained about the abbreviated menu offered today.

After explaining about Em, these customers and the rest of the lunch crowd that followed were only too happy to order simple hamburgers and salads, or a fried fish platter that Clark had pulled together.

By two o'clock the last of the lunch clientele left. Slade was pleased with the way things had run but knew he had to tell Nicole what he'd done. He picked up his phone and got her number from Clark. He swallowed, hoping Nicole wouldn't have him arrested for being in the restaurant without her permission.

~

Nicole parked her Jeep behind her café and opened the back door. Clark was at the grill working on a couple of hamburgers.

He turned. "Nicole, what are you doing here?"

"I could ask you the same thing, but since Mr. Larson took it on himself to open up for me, I guess I know." She walked up to him. "Thank you for doing this. I know it wasn't easy for you."

"Honestly, it wasn't a big deal. We offered the simple stuff on the menu and no one complained."

She swallowed a lump in her throat then nodded.

When she walked out into the dining room, she stopped to watch Slade carry two drinks to a table. He placed them down, talked with the customers, then went to another table and straightened the center arrangement. When he turned around, he immediately saw her behind the counter. At first he looked startled, but then he smiled and walked to her.

He raised his hands. "I know you don't approve. You made that perfectly clear on the phone, but people kept coming in and we just couldn't close."

Nicole looked at the couple sitting with their drinks.

She waved to them and smiled. "That's Harry and Susan. They're loyal locals. You couldn't have sent them away had you tried."

"So you forgive me?" He raised his eyebrow.

"Of course I forgive you. You went beyond the call of duty by doing this. I'll never be able to pay you back."

"I don't want to be paid back." He stopped and raised his eyebrow again. "No wait. Maybe there is one thing you can do."

Nicole frowned but listened.

"You can forget I was a jock in high school and give me another chance to get to know you without that hanging over our heads."

Nicole let out a big breath. "I think I can do that."

"Great. Now why don't you go back home and be with that little girl of yours? Clark and I can handle this."

"I'm touched. I truly am, but Miss Tillie is with Em for about an hour. I feel okay to leave her for a little while. I want to help. I can help Clark get ready for the dinner hour."

Nicole walked over and visited with Susan and her husband. Both were concerned about Em. After lots of hugs and good wishes, Nicole assured them she'd call if she needed help. She worked in the kitchen for a little while, then realized Clark and Slade had the restaurant under control. Word had gotten out in her neighborhood about Em, and several of her neighbors called to insist they help Miss Tillie with Em the next day so she could return to the restaurant.

I am so blessed.

She walked out into the dining room and watched

Slade work the small crowd as if Tony's Place was a fancy, big city establishment. He looked at home with the apron tied around his waist as he carried drinks and food to the customers. He was suave and friendly, carried himself with assurance, and talked to the small-town customers as if they were his long-time friends. Nicole didn't know what his real career involved, but she was sure it wasn't waiting on customers in a small café.

Nicole passed a cloth across the already clean countertop. She knew she had to get back home so Miss Tillie could get some rest, but she hated leaving her little café. She'd always loved the atmosphere here. She enjoyed cooking and relished the visits she had with those that dropped in, and today proved to her what she had decided years ago. This little town was home. In spite of the fact that she had no family here, she felt she belonged.

A tear threatened to fall down her cheek. She swiped it away and plastered a smile on her face. This was a good day. These were good people around her, and for the first time in a long time, she knew she and Em would survive without Tony.

~

For the next few days, Nicole opened the restaurant as usual. Sometimes Em stayed with her and played with her dolls away from the customers or worked on her schoolwork, and sometimes Miss Tillie or one of the neighbors stayed at the house with her. Finally the doctor cleared her to return to school. It seemed life was on the right track. More customers seemed to find their way to the café, and at the end of each day, Nicole had to smile with the cash registers totals.

Everything seemed to be good, but she had to admit that one thing was missing. Slade hadn't called or come by since the day he'd kept the restaurant open for her. She thought about calling him, but talked herself out of doing it.

What would she say? She'd already thanked him.

No. She decided to take care of her daughter, run her restaurant, and accept the fact that Slade Larson had done her a favor with no strings attached.

Several days later as she opened for the lunch customers, she found Slade standing on the sidewalk.

"Slade? Why are you standing here? Why didn't you knock?"

"I saw you rushing around trying to get things ready for lunch and I didn't want to bother you."

"For the man who worked a full day here, you are welcomed here any time."

"Great. Glad you feel that way."

Nicole stepped aside. "Come on in. What can I get you?"

"I'm not here to eat. I had to fly home for a few days, but I'm back helping Mac out again and I promised him I'd work in our restaurant today."

Nicole's mind was spinning not sure why he was here in her café.

Slade lifted a hand to Clark who looked out the kitchen window, then he looked directly at Nicole. "Mac told me that Em is doing okay, so I was wondering if you have any plans when you get off work. I'd love to buy you a cup of coffee or eat a little something and sit and talk. If you don't want to leave Em, you can even bring her along."

Now Nicole's mind almost spun out of control. He

was asking her out. Was this a date? She hadn't been out with anyone since Tony died. She swallowed and took a chance.

"No, I don't have any plans except to get home to Emily, but if Miss Tillie can stay with her a longer long, I'd like to spend a little time with you. I'll check with her and let you know."

"Good. I'll look forward to that." He took a big breath. "Guess I'd better get back to the restaurant before Mac gets upset with me. Let me put my number in your phone so you can call."

Slade said his goodbyes then waved to her again through the window as he walked down the sidewalk.

Nicole sat down and dropped her head into her hands. What had she done?

He'd asked her to spend a little time with him. It was just for a drink. It wasn't a real date. Still, being alone with a man in any social situation was difficult for her to do.

You're being ridiculous. We're not going out for a formal dinner. Just a drink.

She pulled her phone out of her pocket and stared at it for a moment. Should she simply lie and tell him Miss Tillie couldn't watch Emily?

No, she wouldn't do that. Pulling in a big breath, she called her house.

Just a drink. That's all.

Nicole finished the dinner shift trying not to think about being with Slade a little later. He'd told her he'd walk from Slade's to meet her and they could decide what they wanted to do.

As she gathered her things to leave, she saw him walk past the window. Just seeing him brought a smile to her face.

He walked through the door. "Are you still working?"

"Nope, I'm ready. Since you walked, do you want to stay in the neighborhood? We could go to The Yellow Rooster. I hear there's a great singer on the weekends."

"Uh, no, let's take a ride across the bridge and sit at one of the front beach restaurants."

"Ok. That'll be great."

"I know you have a Jeep. I would be honored if you'd let me drive it."

"You can certainly drive my Jeep, but don't expect it to be very luxurious. It's old and well worn."

"Nothing wrong with 'well worn.'"

She grabbed her purse and with his arm on her elbow, they walked out the back door. When they got to the car, Slade opened the passenger door. She hesitated slightly then climbed in. Nicole closed her eyes. Her heart pounded. What was she doing? She didn't know this man. Even though she'd cried all over his nice dress shirt when they'd gotten Em home from the hospital, she really didn't know anything about him except for vague memories from high school and the fact that he was Mac's brother.

She watched him walk around the front of the vehicle, rubbing his hand on the hood. In a moment he'd be driving Tony's Jeep.

That thought almost did her in

Slade slipped into the seat, slammed his door, then he turned to her and smiled that devastating smile she'd seen only a couple of times. She smiled back. She'd deal with those thoughts of Tony when she was back at her house.

"I haven't driven anything like this in years," he said, obviously not knowing her thoughts had drifted to Tony. "I hope I don't knock you around too much trying to remember how to drive a shift."

She cleared her head of any thoughts. Anything materialized in her head right now would make no sense so she tried to enjoy herself. "I'm sure it'll come back to you, but to be on the safe side, I'll hold on."

"Thanks for the encouragement." He chuckled as he started the engine, backed out of the parking lot and smoothly pulled onto the narrow street.

"See. You haven't forgotten."

"This is great! I feel like a kid again."

From Nicole's side of the car she watched him. The serious man she'd been with a couple of times before was gone and in his place was a carefree man with a cute smile on his face, the same smile she remembered from high school.

"I have a car in New York, but it lives in a downtown garage," he said as he pulled out onto the main road that would take them to the bay bridge. "I live just a few blocks from my work so I usually flag down a cab or walk if the weather's good. I don't get to drive around much."

"So you live in New York City?"

"Yep. Right smack in the middle of the business district."

"Do you like living in all that chaos?"

He glanced over at her. "I wouldn't call it chaos. It's definitely crowded, but I avoid Times Square and places where the tourists go. I have a great selection of nice restaurants and clubs near me, so I guess I'm pretty territorial." He chuckled. "Or maybe just plain boring."

"Compared to my life, I certainly wouldn't call you boring. I can see you frequenting the museums and theater and all those wonderful restaurants."

"For sure the city has a lot to offer. I don't take advantage of everything like I should, but I used to."

They crossed the bridge. Nicole closed her eyes and relished the warm breeze blowing through her hair. "I never get to do this. I seem to always be heading someplace in a hurry or working."

Slade looked at her. "Glad you're enjoying yourself."

Without much conversation, they headed down Biloxi's front beach, then drove to an area the locals call Restaurant Row. Slade pulled into a parking lot.

"Gosh, I haven't been here in years," she said. "Tony and I used to come here, but the restaurants aren't the same. This one looks new."

Slade turned in his seat. His expression serious. "I'm sure you miss Tony."

"Yes. He's been gone about three years now."

"I'm sorry," he said low, then opened his door.

She didn't wait for him to open her door, but he was next to her side of the Jeep before she got out. He held the door and offered her his hand. She followed him up the elevator then stood quietly as he asked for a table overlooking the Mississippi Sound and the beach. It was exactly what she hoped it would be.

And Slade was exactly as she thought he'd be as well, a perfect gentleman as he led her through the restaurant and out onto the porch.

Since she'd become a widow, Nicole was in control of everything in her life. It was nice to let someone else take the lead.

"Are you hungry? You can order anything you'd like," he asked as he pulled out a chair for her.

"I am but I was only planning on getting a quick drink. I don't want to take advantage of Miss Tillie."

"I'll ask them to rush the order. I didn't think I was hungry, but now that I smell their fried seafood, I don't think I can pass on the fried shrimp. How about I get one order for us to split?"

He placed the food order then added two mojitos.

"Make mine light," Nicole threw in. When the waitress walked away, she added, "I can't forget I have to spend time with Em tonight. I promised we'd read a new book together."

"I understand, and I admire you for always putting your daughter first."

"Every working single mother does what I do. It's not special."

"Oh, no, it's very special."

"I feel privileged to be able to do it for Em. She's excited about learning. I have to keep donating books. She has more than I can store." She sat up straighter and changed the subject. "So, what exactly is your job in the big city?"

He seemed to hesitate before answering. "I work in finance."

"That's pretty broad. Is that in a bank?"

"Not really. I work with banks, but I also work with businesses that need help trying to survive or need to liquidate. Some people call what I do an investment broker or a merger and acquisitions company."

She wondered if he knew the investment company that had bought her building that was now The Yellow

Rooster but the waitress brought their drinks before she had time to ask.

"This looks refreshing. Thanks."

Slade took a sip. "This is great. I ordered one of these at a local lounge in New York. The bartender made a really good one, but sitting in the middle of a crowded lounge wasn't the same as sitting in the open air on a warm Gulf Coast evening."

"Why, Mr. Larson, that's very poetic."

"You mean for a jock?"

"No, not for a jock." She laughed along with him. "I have to agree though. I'm sure this drink was made for a place like this."

"Before the waitress came you were telling me about your work. It seems as though with your background you'll be able to help out Mac with his business."

"I hoped there would be a simple solution for the lounge, but I might be too close to the business. I can't swoop in and change everything. He's my brother and I might add, my partner. I still own a small part."

"You never wanted to live here?"

"This is where Mac and I were raised, and after Dad died I tried to make a go of it. I had always worked there while Dad owned it, but when he died, it was different. It was as if I had a choice to make with my life. Mac loved running the place, but it's not the life for me or at least it wasn't at the time. I saw what that lifestyle had done to my family, and I made the choice not to be part of it." He took a sip. "I have a feeling Mac still resents me for moving."

"He shouldn't hold that against you. People have to do what's best for themselves."

"So is that why you stay here?"

She thought a moment before answering. As she noted earlier, she really didn't know this man so didn't want to blurt out her entire personal life. "I love living here. I'd love to raise Emily here like her dad wanted."

"I know you said your mom lives in Tennessee. Do you see her often?"

"Not really. She'd love for us to live up there, but it would make Mom's life much more difficult than it is now." She took a sip. "She's begging me to go up for Christmas."

"And?"

"And I told her it can't be this year. It's only in Tennessee but it might as well be across the globe. Funds are a little tight right now. I'm struggling to pay medical insurance and . . . I'm sorry. You don't need to hear all that."

"I'm sorry for more reasons than one. It's a shame our restaurants can't get together to get health insurance."

"That would be wonderful, but that's the nature of the game. I understand how it all works."

"How about Tony's family? Do they live anywhere close?"

"They still try to be part of Em's life, but they're in northern New York and have lots of other grandkids. They offered to move us up there but I really don't think I'd feel comfortable. We never had the chance to get close before Tony passed away, and I'm not sure how the cold winters would affect Em."

"It must be hard having a sick child and no family here."

He has no idea how hard it is.

She looked everywhere but in his eyes. "Yes," is all she managed to say.

Several couples with children stepped out onto the porch and sat near the back. Both she and Slade watched a little boy with dark brown hair crawl up on a seat by himself.

"Cute little boy." Slade's eyes glistened as he watched the child.

Nicole, too, watched him. The boy's dark hair reminded her of Tony. He'd always wanted a son, and Nicole was sure had they had one he would have the same coloring as this child, just as their Em had.

Slade turned his attention back to her. "I know Miss Tillie is a life saver for you. My dad really respected her husband. 'Now, that's a good man,' he used to say, so if Miss Tillie is anywhere as nice as he was, I know you have found a jewel in her."

"Yes, she's definitely a jewel." Nicole took a sip as well. "This is good. I'm glad you talked me into coming."

"I'm glad you came too. I'd like for you to know I'm no longer like those jocks you knew in high school." He laughed. "We all thought we were so cool. Who knew some of our fellow students thought we were crude and uncouth?"

"That's a little harsh." This time she laughed. "Well, maybe not. I guess some of us nerds felt that way because we were the brunt of so many jokes."

"That hurts. We would've never done anything to hurt anyone just because they weren't part of the kids we ran with."

"I beg to differ."

"Excuse me?" He leaned back in his chair. "Oh, no,

I'm about to get shot down, right?"

Nicole really didn't want to talk about the humiliation she felt when she realized her secret admirer letter was a prank.

"No, I'm not striking back tonight. Let's just say some of your friends were not very kind to us who lived in science labs, libraries, and music rooms."

Slade surprised her. He reached across the table and took her hand. "Mac reminded me that you were the recipient of a fake secret admirer letter. I want you to know I had nothing to do with that. I remember the guys laughing about it in the field house one day. I laughed too. I guess I wasn't brave enough to stand up against an entire room of fellow jocks. I'm sorry. I should've done something, but at the time I didn't even know you."

"You have nothing to be ashamed of."

"Yes, I do. I stood back and let a fellow student get hurt. Forgive me?"

"Yes, I think we've already established I wouldn't hold your jock status against you."

The waitress brought out a plate of golden brown fried butterfly shrimp.

"Oh, this looks wonderful."

They quit talking and ate their shrimp. Nicole watched Slade eat and imagined him dressed in his suits attending Broadway plays or heading up important business meetings. Yet, he looked as comfortable as she was sitting at an outside table with seagulls flying around them begging for food.

Slade Larson was a man with many sides. For a fleeting moment she wished she could get to know all of what made him tick, but including a man in her life now wasn't in the equation. Emily was her priority.

"You do know I now owe you twice," she said in spite of her previous thoughts about not getting involved with any man right now.

"What?"

"Twice. You took care of us at the hospital and then tonight. I guess I need to cook you a meal."

Slade smiled and Nicole had to swallow. Tony had been a handsome man, but Slade—wow—his smile nearly did her in.

"You should never offer a home cooked meal to a bachelor. I'm all in."

"Then it's on. You name the day and Emily and I will treat you to a meal at our humble abode, but Sundays are my only day off."

Slade smiled again. "That humble abode, as you call it, is a little piece of heaven to someone who lives in a flat in New York City."

Chapter Six

Nicole got home about an hour later than usual, but Emily was still awake. She and Miss Tillie sat on the porch together, and when Emily saw Nicole she jumped up and ran to the top of the steps.

"Mama, look what we did." Emily held up a paper with beans and noodles pasted on it.

Nicole hurried up the front steps. "Why, Em, that's beautiful. You made a flower using beans."

"And noodles," Emily shouted and jumped up and down in place.

"I love it." Nicole did love the picture but she loved seeing Emily feeling so great today. "Now who showed you how to do that?"

Emily giggled. "It was Miss Tillie. She said she used to make bean art when she was in school. Did you know Miss Tillie used to go to school and was a little girl like me?"

"I sure did." Nicole leaned over and got her evening hug, holding her a little longer than usual. She kissed her daughter on the forehead, then took the pasted bean and noodle picture and examined it. "When I was a little girl like you, I used to do this too, but I'd forgotten all about doing it. I'm so glad Miss Tillie showed you how. You can remind me sometimes when we have nothing to do, and we can make our own bean art."

Nicole looked over at Miss Tillie. "Thanks. I know she enjoyed this, and I really hope you didn't mind staying a little longer."

"Oh, heavens no. We had fun." She stood up. "And what about you? Did you and that gorgeous Mr. Larson have a good time?"

"Now, Miss Tillie, we just talked." But Nicole couldn't hide her smile. "But, yes, it was fun."

"You call me anytime. I'd love to see you go out once in a while."

Nicole was about to tell Miss Tillie she wasn't ready to go out with anyone, but she realized she'd made a tentative date to cook for Slade.

Would that be considered at date? How would she feel by allowing Slade into her home once again and have him share an evening meal with them?

Miss Tillie stepped next to her and touched her arm. "Nicole, you know it's okay to have a little fun and an actual life. I can help you with Emily if you decide to go out—and I hope you do especially if it's with Slade Larson. He comes from a hard-working family."

Nicole smiled as Miss Tillie turned to go down the steps. "Thank you, but you do know Slade is only here on the coast temporarily. Nothing can come of it."

"That doesn't mean you can't enjoy his company while he's here, and who knows what might happen?"

Nicole shook her head and laughed. "See you

tomorrow."

"Bye, Miss Tillie." Em shouted and waved. "Mama, can we hang my picture on the refrigerator?"

"Of course. I think that's a great place for it."

She followed Em into the house. As she passed the phone in the hallway, she ignored the blinking message light. She'd listen to it later. If it was her mom, she'd call her back, but if it was another call from Barry Keats, she'd have to decide how to handle it. She knew she was responsible for Tony's debts, but she had no idea how she could pay the large payment the man wanted right now. A little extension would help. With the additional business in the restaurant last week, she hoped she could work something out with him.

The next several days went smoothly for her. The message had not been from Barry, but from her mother. The conversation with her later that night eased Nicole's nerves. More than anything she wished she could feel her mother's arms around her, but she knew that wasn't possible. Not now anyway. Once again her mom asked them to consider coming up for Christmas.

It broke Nicole's heart to tell her she couldn't afford it, but there was no way she could spend money on a plane ticket when so many other debts loomed over her head.

Besides the large debt she owed Mr. Keats she had to keep money in the bank to pay for emergencies with Emily. One day she'd have to take her someplace for more specialized treatments and she would need money to do that. Her little girl was priority and if she had to sell everything she had, she'd make sure Em would get what she needed.

During the next week more and more customers

seemed to find their way to Nicole's café. She was thrilled. On Saturday morning when she was working on the stuffed crab special of the day, she was surprised to see Mac waving to her through the front window.

"Mac, this is such a nice surprise," she said as she opened the door. "Come on in."

Mac gave her a brotherly hug. "You're looking great and I hear business is picking up."

"It is. I couldn't be happier."

"We seem to be having a few good weeks as well. Let's hope business keeps looking up."

"Now, what do I have the pleasure of your company this morning?"

"I haven't seen you in a while and my little brother seems to mention your name every day. I couldn't let him have one up on me. Thought I'd come see you so I could add to his conversation."

Nicole felt her face flush. "Your brother was a lifesaver for Em and me when she ended up in the hospital."

"He is really touched by Em. I've never pictured my brother with children, but I swear he is falling in love with your daughter. Of course, who wouldn't?"

"That's sweet of you to say. When you see him today would you ask him to call me? I promised to cook a meal for him for all he did for us. I'd like to do it this coming Sunday if he's even going to be in town."

Mac straightened his back and put his hands on his hips. "Cook for him? Do you know we've known each other for years, and you've never offered this bachelor a meal? I think I'm jealous."

Nicole laughed. "There's a simple remedy for that. If you and Slade can get away from the restaurant on

Sunday, you can come over with him and I'll feed both of you."

"Sounds great. We'll let you know."

Nicole headed back to her kitchen feeling relieved. Having both the Larson brothers in her home for a meal was something she could handle.

It would not be a date.

Nicole's day went quickly and by the time she walked into the dining area to lock up, she was surprised to see Slade sitting at a table. Her heart fluttered.

"I hope you're not too hungry. The kitchen is closed."

"Nope, not hungry at all. Just thought I'd catch you before you left. I've been so busy since I got back from New York I haven't had time to come see how things are going down here and with Em."

"Things are going great. I've had a really good week." She walked to the front door and locked it then grabbed her purse. "Mind walking out the back with me? If you didn't drive, I'll drop you off at Mac's."

"No, the short walk is great. I love walking along the bay road."

She led him through the kitchen and out the back door. After locking up Slade walked her to her Jeep. A thin haze settled around the street lamp. As they got to her Jeep, Slade leaned up against it instead of opening her door.

Nicole dug into her purse for her keys, but Slade didn't step away.

"I lied," he said. "I did want to see about Em and about how your business was going, but," he grinned, "I really just wanted to see you."

Her hands stopped. Did she want to hear those words? Could she allow herself to enjoy his attention?

"Nicole, did you hear me? I said I wanted to see you. I've enjoyed being with you the few times we've had together. I'd like to have another opportunity. Maybe have a real date."

She bit her lip.

Slade crossed his arms. "But I get the feeling you don't want to do that."

Nicole found her voice. "I don't know how I feel."

"That's not hard. You either want to see me again or not."

"No, Slade, it's not that easy. I've enjoyed our time together, but I don't know if I can find time to be a normal single woman. I have a restaurant to run and a sick child and," she hesitated, "you're just passing through here."

"Is that the only reasons?"

Nicole held her breath. Of course that wasn't the only reason, but how could she tell him she didn't know if she was ready to go out with another man. Tony had been the only man she'd ever wanted to be with.

"Nicole?" his crooked smile made her smile. "Hey, you in there?"

"I'm sorry. I guess I was in deep thought. You've given me a lot to think about."

"Maybe that's a good thing."

She looked down. "Maybe. Maybe not."

Slade pushed away from the Jeep. "Okay, I give up. If not a date, will you still cook me a meal? You promised, remember?"

Again, his smile was devastating.

"Sure. I'll be glad to. I saw Mac and invited him as

well. Or maybe he invited himself, but I'll be glad to cook for both of you this coming Sunday. Would that be okay?"

"Sunday would be great, but with Mac? You mean I have to bring my big brother along?" He took a step toward her and placed his hands on her shoulders. "Okay, I'll bring my brother if that's the only way I can get a meal."

She slid onto her seat.

Slade closed her door. "I look forward to enjoying a home cooked meal with you and Em." He rolled his eyes. "And my brother."

She lifted her hand in a goodbye as she drove away. In her rearview mirror she saw he had not moved, but watched her. She was glad he couldn't see her huge smile.

~

Sunday afternoon turned out to be the day everyone agreed upon for their meal together. Early Saturday morning before she went to the café, she and Em walked the aisles of the local supermarket finding just the right ingredients for her Italian dinner she planned to serve. Since Mac's restaurant served mostly seafood dishes, she wanted to cook something different. Tony had been a great cook and taught her some of his mother's recipes.

"Look, Mama." Em held up a bright red tomato. "Can we have some of these?"

"Yep. You have a good eye, Miss Em. Pick out two more to go with that one and I'll find the rest of the vegetables for the salad."

She examined each piece as she put them in her wagon, then moved next to Em who was still trying to find just the right tomatoes.

"I think these are just fine."

Em scrunched her lips. "I want them to be beautiful and perfect. I want Mr. Mac and Mr. Slade to like what we cook them."

"I guarantee they will love our meal. What man could resist our homemade tomato sauce with the big beef roast cooked in it with our salad and hot Italian bread? Your daddy used to say any man would fall in love with a meal like that."

As soon as the words tumbled from her mouth, she regretted them and hoped Em wasn't paying too close attention.

"My daddy used to say that?" she asked. "I don't remember."

"It's okay not to remember. I'll remind you all the time what he used to say about the things we did. That way you won't forget."

Em smiled big, finished picking out the tomatoes, then handed them to Nicole. "Maybe our meal will make Mr. Mac or Mr. Slade fall in love with us and one of them will be my new daddy."

Nicole swallowed, not sure how to handle such an innocent statement filled with such heavy implication.

"We want them to love our food and I think they will." She hoped that would move the conversation along.

It didn't.

"But I want them to love us too, Mama. I like them. It would be fun if one of them wanted to be my daddy."

Nicole put the tomatoes in the basket, then squatted down by her daughter. "Em, honey, one day we might find you a new daddy, but right now we just need some new friends. Would that be okay?"

Em frowned. "I guess."

"Good. Now let's go find our favorite bread and decide what we'll fix for dessert."

"Cake and ice cream!" Em shouted.

"Okay, I can do that." Cake and ice cream wasn't one of the desserts Nicole had thought about, but if Em wanted that, she'd buy a small cake and still make one of the cobblers she'd thought about doing. That way everyone would be happy.

Happy.

Would her life ever lend itself to happiness again?

But then she only had to watch her daughter skip through the aisle of the supermarket to know what true happiness was.

With all the ingredients for their dinner bought, Nicole helped Em into the Jeep then reached for the bags of groceries.

"Mrs. Russo. I thought that was you."

Nicole cringed. She'd recognize that voice anywhere.

"Em, you stay in the car. I have to talk to this man." She closed the door, forced a smile on her face, then looked at the man she hoped had moved to Siberia or someplace as far away from the Gulf Coast as possible.

"Mr. Keats, how are you? I didn't expect to run into you at the supermarket."

"Neither did I, but I did expect to hear from you since I've left several messages on your phone."

Nicole knew she wasn't a good fibber, but she tried. "Yes, I did get one of them, but that was during the time my daughter ended up in the hospital. I guess I forgot about you when things finally calmed down in my life. I'm so sorry."

Barry Keats didn't say anything. He stared at her with pale blue eyes that made Nicole look away. Except for his ruddy skin and the eyes, he was a decent looking man, but Nicole knew he wasn't someone she could trust and definitely not someone to ignore.

"Mr. Keats, I'm really trying to come up with the money." She swallowed. "Business at the restaurant is picking up, so I was planning to get with you soon. I don't have a decent sum to offer you right now, but I will shortly. I know we talked about what kind of payments you want, but I was going to ask if we could revise the payment plan with smaller amounts. It's hard for me to come up with big sum like we agreed to."

"That's not my concern. I'm a businessman and my business depends on people living up to their promises. Your husband signed for a huge loan to help fix up that building he bought. I'm sorry it didn't work out for you two, but there's nothing I can do but demand my money back and not in tiny payments. The interest is compounding daily. The longer you wait, the harder it will be for you to repay the loan. Not repaying is out of the question. You have that Jeep and a house right in the middle of what might be some of the most valuable land around here soon. This area is growing by leaps and bounds. I will get my money one way or the other, and believe me the courts will back me up."

"Mama, let's go. I'm hot." Em had opened the door and stuck her head out. "Come on."

"And that little girl," said Keats with a smirk on his face. "She's really cute. She needs a house to live in, doesn't she?"

Nicole stepped between her little girl leaning out the

window and Keats. Her blood boiled. "I'll get your money to you, but leave my family alone."

Keats chuckled. "Your husband didn't think much of his family to put you in such a bind, did he?"

Nicole turned to leave, but Keats stepped in front of her. "Mrs. Russo, I'm not a mean person, but I am a businessman as I told you. I have to have payment on that loan. The law will back me up if I demand you give me that Jeep or your house as payment. I'd hate for you to have to depend on walking or catching a taxi, but I don't know what else to do, do you?"

"As I told you, I'm trying, and I'm sure I can start a payment plan to get the loan down."

"And as I said, the interest is going to make those payments sky-high. You've got to come up with a lump sum, not a few pennies here and there."

"Please give me more time. I'll come up with something soon."

"Very soon." He lifted his hand as if he were tipping a hat to her, spun around and left her standing in the parking lot. Her body shook knowing there was no way could she come up with enough money to satisfy him.

Chapter Seven

On Sunday after church, Nicole scurried around her kitchen with a smile on her face getting ready for Mac and Slade to come over for an early dinner. Their visit would be a nice reprieve to get her mind off the meeting with Keats at the supermarket yesterday. She'd tossed and turned until late into the night thinking about the financial problem she faced with the man.

She tried really hard not to be mad at Tony for putting her in this situation, but it didn't help. She wanted to scream, or cry, or curse, but that would never do with Em in the next room.

When she finally slipped off to sleep about two-thirty, the only possible resolution she'd come up with was to visit one of the local banks to apply for a loan, a loan she knew she could never get since she had so little to put up against it.

She did consider asking Tony's dad or one of his uncles for a loan. Both of them could afford to help her and wondered why Tony had not gone to them instead of getting involved with someone like Barry Keats. Since Tony must've had his reasons for not approaching his family, she decided they would be her last resort as well.

But facing Keats without some kind of money to offer was not an option either. She needed her vehicle and the house was legally in her mother's name. She could never turn it over to the man even if she wanted.

Today, though, she'd pushed aside thoughts of Keats and concentrated on her tomato sauce and her blueberry cobbler. She lifted the lid on the big pot on the stove. Breathing in the aroma of simmering tomato sauce always brought back memories of Tony. He had taught her how to make the sauce from recipes he remembered from his mother and grandmother. Those first few meals they cooked together involved endless telephone conversation with the women in his family to make sure he remembered correctly.

Now making the sauce was second nature to her, but it still brought a deep sense of longing that pulled at her heart.

"Mama, can I wear my special dress for dinner tonight?"

Nicole looked over. Em stood inside the kitchen door holding a yellow dress with lace and ribbons she'd worn for her last birthday. She'd seen it in a store window and begged for Nicole to buy it. When Nicole checked the price, she had to shake her head. It had been way more than she could afford, but the next day Nicole had gone back and asked if she could put the dress on lay-away.

Now she was glad she had done that.

"Today's special, Mama. With Mr. Mac and Mr.

Slade here with us I have to wear something special." She stopped and scrunched her lips. "How come Miss Tillie isn't coming?"

"I invited her, but she said she wanted to eat earlier, but we'll take her a plate afterwards."

"Ok. She can see my dress when we go over."

Nicole walked over to Em, squatted down by her, and placed both hands on her arms. "Yes she can. I'm glad you want to wear that dress, but you have to wear something over it while we eat so you don't ruin it."

"You mean a bib? You want me to wear a baby bib?"

"No, not a bib, just something to protect your dress."

"Will you wear something in front of yours too?"

Nicole laughed. "Yes, I'll put something over my clothes."

"Mr. Mac and Mr. Slade needs to do that too. They don't want to leave with spots on their clothes either."

"We can certainly offer, but we won't insist if they don't want to. We don't want our company to feel uncomfortable."

Em was satisfied. She spun around then ran from the kitchen.

By five o'clock Em shrieked. "Mama, they're here."

Nicole looked around the kitchen, then down at her clothes, decided she was ready, then headed into the living room. Em had already opened the door.

"We've been waiting for you. Look at my dress. It's special." Em spun around. "Today is special. Mama said I could wear it if I cover it when I eat."

Mac and Slade stood outside on the porch with smiles on their faces listening to Em babble about her dress. Slade stooped down. "Now that certainly is a special dress. You look like a princess."

"Mama, did you hear that? He said I look like a princess."

Nicole walked up to them and smiled at the two tall handsome men talking with her daughter. "Please, come in."

Slade stood up. Mac held out a small bouquet of flowers that Nicole recognized from the local supermarket.

She took the flowers and smiled at the guys. "Thank you so much. Flowers were on my list when I went shopping but somehow I didn't make it home with them."

What she neglected to tell them was she decided the added expense wasn't necessary.

"I know you don't have a lot of time so why don't you follow me into the dining area. Dinner is just about ready."

As she turned, Slade held out a bottle of white wine. "I thought we could have a sip before dinner." His smile nearly did her in.

"You guys think of everything. Yes, that would be great." All the jitters she'd had getting the dinner together for two men in her home vanished at the sight of Slade.

"Come on," Em took Mac's hand. "I'll show you where we're going to eat. We don't sit in here a lot but Mama said tonight was special so we could."

Nicole laughed. "Except for Miss Tillie and my music students, we don't get a lot of company any more so we were both thrilled to be able to set the dining table instead of the small table in the kitchen."

"I helped set the table."

Slade stopped walking and looked down at Em. "We could use someone like you at Mr. Mac's restaurant. You are a big help."

"I am. Mama says that all the time." Again Em lifted the skirt of her dress and spun around.

Everyone laughed.

"I need to check on the dinner, and I'll put those flowers in a vase so we can enjoy them." She looked at Slade. "If you'd like to open the wine and pour, everything you need is right here in the hutch." She stepped nearer to the hutch and found a crystal vase, a wedding gift from one of Tony's aunts. Looking at the vase reminded her she might have to call them for a loan, but she ignored the dread that shot though her and looked up at the guys. "I'll get these flowers arranged."

Nicole left the two men in the dining room with Em entertaining them with stories about what Miss Tillie and she did during the week. Nicole put some water in the vase, clipped the stems on the flowers then arranged them. After checking the sauce and turning the oven to preheat, she grabbed some salad toppings to put on the table with one hand and the vase of flowers with the other.

Slade met her at the door. "Do you need some help? We were a little tied up listening to Em, and I didn't get in here to help."

"No, but thank you."

Slade placed a hand on her elbow and let her slide past him into the dining room. As she passed through the door, her right side rubbed against his chest sending a streak of heat through her body.

She swallowed. "Tight door." She looked up and

Slade smiled.

Amazingly tight, she thought, blew out a big breath, then moved into the safe zone of the dining area where she had to stop and chuckle.

Em stood next to Mac talking as fast as Nicole had heard her in a long time. Mac sat facing Em with his wine glass on the table.

Slade stepped next to her. "Here, let me give you a hand with that." He took the vase from her. "On the hutch?"

"Perfect," she said. Smiling, she nodded and looked at her daughter. Em had said this was a special day and as far as Nicole was concerned, it was more than special. It was perfect.

For the next few minutes, everyone sat at the table and relaxed as they sipped their wine. Even Em had a plastic wine glass filled with juice. The conversation centered around the workweek and of course what Em and Miss Tillie did all week.

For the moment Nicole felt free of money and health worries and enjoyed the company. She'd forgotten what it was like to socialize with other adults and actually relax.

As much as she hated to leave the great company at the table, she slipped into the kitchen and put the bread in the oven. When she returned to get it, Slade followed her.

"Tell me what to carry. I'm a good grunt."

"Thanks, Slade. Grunts are always nice to have in the kitchen."

He walked to the stove. "You've been a busy lady. This smells wonderful."

"Let's hope it tastes as good as it smells."

He grabbed two potholders, then lifted one of the dishes warming in the oven. "This bachelor's stomach is growling."

"Good. I hope you leave full." She lifted a dish as well and together they walked into the dining area.

When Nicole returned to the kitchen for a bowl of vegetables, she leaned against the counter and thought how much she enjoyed having the men here, especially Slade. She'd forgotten what it was like to have visitors in her house, especially men who made her feel like a woman again.

So many feelings bombarded her brain. "I'll deal with them later," she said to herself and picked up the last bowl and headed to the small dining area. When she stepped into the room she stopped and had to hold back a giggle. Both men and Em sat at the table with yellow linen napkins around their necks. Slade looked up and winked at her sending a streak of warmth through her body.

Not wanting to acknowledge what his wink had done to her, she put the bowl of pasta down and took a napkin that Em handed to her.

"This one's for you, Mama."

"Thank you." She tucked the napkin around her neck. Both men grinned, then bowed their heads as Em recited a short grace.

Nicole had wondered how she would keep the conversation going with two men she hardly knew, but Em solved that problem. She talked excitedly throughout the meal, and when it was time for dessert, she insisted on helping Nicole bring in the ice cream and the small cake they'd picked out from the supermarket deli.

Nicole went back for the cobbler, then sat down to serve.

"Please, help yourselves," Nicole said as she scooped ice cream on Em's cake. "I think I'll save mine for later. I'm stuffed."

"I am too," said Slade, "but I have to taste that cobbler."

She served him a small bowl with a little ice cream on it.

"I'm stuffed too," said Mac, "but I'm not passing on this. I can't tell you the last time I had homemade cobbler." He served himself a huge bowl with ice cream, then sat back and ate along with Em.

"You're a lucky girl, Miss Em, if you get to eat like this all the time."

"I am, huh? Miss Tillie usually cooks for us when Mama is working and she cooks just as good as Mama does."

Mac was digging into his cobbler when his phone range. He swallowed, then excused himself and answered the phone as he walked out the room.

"Hope nothing is wrong at the restaurant." Slade finished the last spoon of his cobbler, then looked toward the door.

"Well, guys, I've got to run," Mac said as he walked back into the dining room. "My bartender has to leave early and he's making sure I remembered." Mac pulled his napkin from around his neck, then looked at Nicole. "I can't tell you how much I've enjoyed this. I hate to eat and run, but I have to go."

"I understand. I'm glad you got to join us. I'll send some cobbler for the two of you with Slade when he leaves."

Slade looked at Mac. "Do you need me at the restaurant?"

"No, but thanks for offering. I'll call you if things change."

They said their goodbyes. Em sat in her chair and waved rather than walking him to the door as she usually did.

Nicole walked over to her and felt her forehead. "Are you feeling okay?"

"I'm tired."

"Why don't you rest in your room while we clean the kitchen?"

Em nodded, then headed to her room.

Slade stood up and started picking up dishes. "Is she okay?"

"I think so. If she doesn't feel like walking down to Miss Tillie's, would you mind taking some dinner for her on your way home?"

"You know I will." He smiled at her, then picked up a few more dishes.

Just as he'd done on the day he'd brought Em home from the hospital, Slade pitched in and carried, then washed and dried dishes. Several times, Nicole walked to Em's room to check on her.

They worked side by side. Nicole told him about her childhood, then thanked him for wearing the napkin around his neck. "I have to say both you and Mac looked really cute."

He laughed. "Wouldn't have had it any other way."

Nicole fixed Miss Tillie a nice sampling from her dinner and placed the plates in a basket. She looked around the kitchen. "Thanks for helping with the dishes. I really don't mind doing them, but now we have time to enjoy the evening a little."

As soon as the words tumbled out of her mouth, she regretted them. "Let me go check on Em to see if she feels like walking to Miss Tillie's." She turned and left the room hoping he didn't see the blush on her face from suggesting they spend more time together.

Em begged to walk down to Miss Tillie's so Nicole relented. Slade didn't mention her comment as the three of them left her house and headed down the sidewalk.

"Miss Tillie, look what we have for you?" Em pulled away from Nicole and skipped up the steps, then threw her arms around Miss Tillie who had gotten up from her rocking chair.

"Looks like Em is feeling better," Nicole said.

"And look at my dress." Em stepped out of the lady's arms and turned around slowly holding her skirt up.

"You are beautiful in that dress, Miss Em. I'm so glad you came to show me."

Nicole and Slade caught up with Em and stepped up on Miss Tillie's porch. "I brought you a taste of our dinner. You've probably eaten already, but it'll be great tomorrow."

"Yes, it will. Would you mind taking it in and putting the plates in the refrigerator?"

As Nicole stepped into the house, Slade leaned against the porch rail. "You and Nicole are so lucky to have homes on this street."

"My husband and I bought this house years ago when property values were really low. Now, I wouldn't want to live anywhere else."

"That's what Nicole says as well."

"And I'm fortunate she wants to stay here and have

me for a neighbor. Life would be really boring if it weren't for Nicole and Em."

"I'm your best friend, huh?" Em hugged Miss Tillie around her legs.

"You certainly are, and I'm lucky to have you."

"What have I missed?" Nicole said as she walked back out with her empty basket.

"Only a confirmation from your daughter that I'm her best friend."

Nicole laughed. "We'll let you get back to your quiet evening. Em, tell Miss Tillie goodnight so we can leave."

"Oh no, Mama. We just got here. Can I stay, Miss Tillie?"

"Sure, but only if your mom says it's okay."

Nicole swallowed. If Em stayed here, she'd be alone with Slade assuming he'd go back to the house with her. Before she could convince herself to turn down her daughter's request, she nodded because she realized she really did want to spend time alone with Slade.

"Okay, but just for a few minutes. Miss Tillie, we'll be on my porch so you can walk her down or I'll come down a little later to get her. She was a little sluggish after dinner, but looks as if she's perked up."

Slade stepped away from the railing. "You're going to love Nicole's pasta dinner. It's fantastic."

Nicole and Slade left Em fluffing her dress out to sit on a rocker.

"You're got a treasure in that lady," said Slade as he walked slowly down the sidewalk.

"I do and I'm thankful she's here. If it wouldn't be for someone like her to help me, Em and I would've had to live someplace else, something I don't want to do."

"And I for one am glad you stayed."

Nicole didn't comment, but his words pleased her. They walked the short block back to Nicole's without saying anymore, but Nicole didn't mind. It was refreshing to walk in silence and enjoy the early evening. Several neighbors sat on their porches and waved to them as they passed, but other than that they were alone.

When they got to her house, Slade turned to her. "Mind if I sit awhile?"

"Sure. I love sitting on my porch this time of day. It's not often I have a free evening so this is perfect. Would you like a cup of coffee?"

"Yeah. I'd like that."

He opened the door for her and with his hand resting lightly on her arm, he followed her into the kitchen. Nicole relished the touch of his hand on her skin. She continually told herself she didn't need a man in her life, but at times like this she knew that wasn't true.

Nicole started a pot of decaf coffee, then turned. Slade was standing inches away from her. She stiffened.

"Sorry. Didn't mean to startle you."

"You didn't. I guess I was in deep thought." She turned around and put her hands on the counter. "Maybe I'm not fit to have a social life. I'm a bore most of the time because I'm always so worried about Em."

Slade stepped up behind her and put his hands on her shoulders. She backed up. Leaning into his hard body sent a warm sensation throughout her.

"You're not a bore. You're a good mother. A fantastic mother."

His breath warmed her neck and chills ran down her back.

And I'm falling so hard for this guy. I'm hopeless.

"I wish I could take away your worries," he said softly.

She pulled in a long breath, then turned to face him. "You have no idea how you take away my worries. When Em and I are with you, you make me feel as if everything is okay." She closed her eyes and wanted this moment to last forever.

"Then that's what I want to do."

The coffee pot made a loud gulping noise. They both laughed.

"Maybe Santa Claus will bring you a new coffee pot."

"I'd have to be exceptionally good to get something like that."

He kissed her on the tip of her nose. "Miss Russo, you've been really, really good."

Nicole stepped away, inhaled deeply, then got them each a cup of coffee. "Let's go back on the porch."

She sat in a one of her rockers. "So when are you going back to New York?"

"I told Mac I'd work through next week. I've been away so long there are quite a few projects I have to finish. Kelli has my schedule full for two months. Mac wants me to come back for Thanksgiving, and I'd really like to make that happen." He took a sip of coffee. "If I can swing coming back down here, I'd really like to have you and Em join us for Thanksgiving dinner. Do you think that might happen?"

Nicole felt herself smile. "I think that could be arranged. I always celebrate the holidays with Miss Tillie, but maybe she could join us."

"That would be perfect. Then it's a date?"

"Sure. I'd like that. Will you and Mac do the cooking?"

"Mac is a divorcee and I'm a bachelor. Nope, not us. Usually he eats with friends or makes reservations at one of the nicer restaurants here. He's not sure which we'll do this year."

"If he wants to cook, Miss Tillie and I would be glad to contribute dishes or I can host it at my house, and I'll do all the cooking."

"Oh no. If we get to celebrate together, I don't want you or Miss Tillie to be stuck in the kitchen. I think a restaurant sounds great."

"Wow, not cooking on Thanksgiving. That would be amazing. If you do Thanksgiving here, I'd like to invite you and Mac to my house the day after. Em calls it her tree day. We get the Christmas tree down and decorate. Even if it's ninety degrees outside, she insists on hot chocolate because that's what she's seen on TV."

"Sounds like a wonderful time. I'll let everyone know if and when I'll be down." He sipped his coffee and seemed to relax. "This is wonderful," he said. "I love a front porch. My grandmother had one in northern Michigan. When we were boys, Mac and I loved going up there. Her porch was our favorite place. It was built up pretty high and we even played under it. It was a great way to spend our summers."

"When I have a hard day at work or if Em has an episode, this is where I get my life back together. I feel as though problems roll off my shoulders when I sit here."

Slade looked at her and smiled. "And I thank you for letting me sit here and get my life back together."

Nicole sat up. "Does that mean you have problems on your shoulders today?"

He didn't answer. He closed his eyes and leaned back against rocker. "Who doesn't have problems?"

She looked at him for a long moment before she took a deep breath and dropped her head back as well and thought about what he'd said. Slade Larson looked so assured and confident she never imagined he had problems.

Maybe his New York business was in trouble or maybe he wasn't finding a solution to help Mac save the restaurant.

"I guess we never know what our friends are going through, do we?" she said. "We seem to all carry around our own problems tucked away where no one else can see them."

Slade sat up. "That's good to hear."

"What? That we all have problems." She sat up straight and looked at him.

He chuckled. "No. It's good to hear you consider me your friend."

~

The smile Nicole gave Slade made him breathe easy. Coastal life was starting to get to him—or maybe it was Nicole and her little girl who were getting to him. He certainly didn't want her to dislike him because of how she remembered him from high school, and if he were honest with himself, he wanted her to be more than a friend.

"Yes, Slade, I consider you a friend."

"Good because I didn't like the way you looked at me the first few times we were together."

"Hey, I had good reason."

He laughed out loud. "I guess." Again, he relaxed. "Just to be clear, I like you better as a friend."

After a few minutes he looked at her again and decided to take a chance.

"Since we have determined you don't hate me anymore, maybe when I come back for Thanksgiving you'd let me take you out on a real date or better yet, how about I take you and Em for an outing next Sunday and then you and I could have dinner afterwards."

Indecision swept across Nicole's face before she answered, but then she smiled. "As a friend?"

"If that's what I have to agree to for a night out with you, yes, as friends."

She looked down at the floor, then back at him. "Okay."

"Great. I'll look forward to it."

Nicole nodded. "I think I should go save Miss Tillie from Em's talking."

"I'll walk with you then head back. I'd like to stay longer, but if Mac is shorthanded, I'd better show up."

Nicole looked at the sky. "I've enjoyed this. It's a gorgeous evening. I didn't even realize it had gotten dark."

Both of them got up and he opened her gate for her. As she walked through it she stopped. A car inched its way down the street and as it got in front of her house, it nearly stopped. The man behind the wheel tipped his head in her direction.

Nicole didn't wave. Instead, she gripped the gate

and watched him drive away.

Slade had never seen the man, but by the look on Nicole's face, she knew him, and she wasn't thrilled he'd slowed down in front of her house. "Nicole, are you okay?"

She nodded. "I guess."

"Do you know that man?"

She nodded but didn't give an explanation.

Slade walked up behind her and put both his hands on her shoulders. "Has that man done something to you?"

Before she answered, she looked at the car again, then hurried out the gate and watched the car as it slowed down by Miss Tillie's yard.

Slade wasn't sure what was transpiring in front of him, but to be on the safe said, he memorized the car tag. He followed Nicole as she hurried toward Miss Tillie's. When she ran up to the porch, his heart went out to Nicole. She pulled her daughter to her body and hugged her.

It wasn't hard to see something wasn't right, but he had a feeling she would never tell him why her relaxing evening had dissolved with the appearance of the man.

Slade watched the car until it disappeared, made sure he had the tag number embedded in his brain, then turned his attention to Nicole and Em. After a quick goodnight to Miss Tillie, they walked back to the house with Em holding his hand, talking nonstop. He tried to be as excited as the little girl was, but it was hard because Nicole walked in complete silence.

Nicole let Em go into the house before she turned to him.

"Nicole, I'm not sure what's going on here, and I

won't ask you to explain if you don't want to, but you need to talk to someone. I'd love it if you chose me to open up to, but if not, someone."

She nodded, but not very convincingly. Her face was strained. Her eyes glistened.

Slade couldn't stand to see her upset. He pulled her close. For a moment he felt her get rigid, but within seconds she leaned into him and clung to his shirt. They had determined they'd be friends, but in his heart he knew he wanted more from her. He wanted to get to know her even though he knew he didn't belong here in Marsh Isles. What he did know was if she had a problem he wanted her to let him help.

"Thank you for being here." She stepped away. "And for being a friend."

"You know I'm here if you need me."

"I think I do."

"What's that supposed to mean?" He crossed his arms in front of his chest.

"You're here right now, but you'll be gone soon. I don't want to get too comfortable depending on you or anyone. I'm used to taking care of myself and Em."

He put his hands on both of her arms. "You're right. I do need to go back to New York, but while I'm here I want to help you if you need anything. Again, I'm not sure what went through your mind when that guy passed, but it doesn't take a genius to know you were upset. I need to know you'll let me or Mac or someone help you if you need it." He wanted to say more, but he kept his thoughts inside. He had a feeling she wasn't ready to hear any of what he had to say. As she'd mentioned, he'd be leaving soon. "Agreed?"

She nodded. "Yes, I'll call you if I need anything.

Promise."

An overwhelming urge to kiss her slammed into his brain.

He dropped his arms and stepped away to cool his body down. Nicole Russo wasn't ready to have a temporary traveler add to her problems— and kissing her would definitely be a problem, even for him.

"See you around?" He tried to make his voice casual, his comment something a friend would say, but when he glanced back at her, he wanted to run back up on the porch and throw his arms around her. Her strained expression tore at his heart.

He reminded himself he wasn't her knight-in-shining armor.

Waving to her, he closed the gate behind him. What he needed to do was to finish his business with Mac and go back to New York before he got too close to Nicole. If he stayed here, she would eventually find out about his owning The Yellow Rooster. It was inevitable, and he didn't want to see her face when she found out. From the beginning he'd had good intentions of telling her, but each time he couldn't bring himself to say the words. He enjoyed her company and wanted her to enjoy his. That tiny piece of information about the restaurant would destroy all he'd worked for with her.

Still, he couldn't make himself leave her street immediately.

Instead of heading to Slade's, he stopped at Miss Tillie's, who was still sitting on the porch. After a casual greeting, he took a seat next to her.

"Do you know the man who slowed down in front of your house a few minutes ago?"

"No, but Nicole certainly does." Miss Tillie sat up

straight in her rocker. "I have a feeling whoever he is he's harassing her about something. She won't confide in me about what's worrying her."

"She won't open up to me either."

"I keep telling her to contact my nephew Billy. He's on the police force, but she won't do it. She says he's harmless, but I'm not so sure."

"She might not want to contact someone, but I can. I don't know what's going on, but I can tell Nicole's uncomfortable. Your nephew might be able to look up the tag and see who the man is and if he has a record."

Miss Tillie grabbed Slade's hand and told him her nephew's complete name. "Thank you. Thank you so much. Nicole is like a daughter to me. I'm so glad you're here to look out for her even if it's for a little while."

Slade wished he could tell her he'd be around long enough to look out for her for a long time, but he knew he wasn't meant to be back on the Gulf Coast.

Chapter Eight

On the following Sunday, Slade parked his car about a half block from Nicole's house to talk with Miss Tillie before picking up Nicole and Em. Miss Tillie sat in her favorite spot on the porch.

He stepped out of his car. "How are you today?"

"For an old woman, I'd say I'm pretty good." She laughed.

Slade walked up to the fence but didn't go in. "I'm taking Nicole and Em to the children's museum and then to front beach if Em is up to it. Thought it would be fun to play tourist. Would you like to join us?"

"That's sweet of you to ask, but no. I'll wait here. Nicole asked me to watch Em a little later. She said something about having dinner with you."

"That's the plan, but you're welcome to join us for the entire day. We'll be passing here in a few minutes. If you change your mind, wave and we'll stop."

"I really do appreciate it, but these old bones would rather sit right here than dodge all those tourists at the beach." She sat up straight. "Did you call my nephew?"

"I did and he said he'd see what he could do. Thanks for giving me his name. He seems like a good guy and wants to help. I'll keep you informed."

"Please do. I'm as concerned about Nicole as you are, and I don't like whatever that man might be doing."

Slade nodded. "I don't either. I hope your nephew can come up with something." He looked toward Nicole's house. "I'd better go get the girls. We'll be back early." Slade wanted to spend the afternoon with Nicole and Em, but he couldn't wait to spend time alone with Nicole later. He could hardly believe she had actually agreed to go out with him.

Miss Tillie waved as he headed toward Nicole's. He wished he could tell Nicole he'd contacted the police, but he knew she'd be upset so he would have to keep a second secret from her.

I'm going to be in big enough trouble if she finds about The Yellow Rooster and now this.

Em opened the door as soon as he stepped on the porch.

"Mr. Slade, we've been waiting. Mama's ready too."

"Great because we don't want to miss a minute of our day. It's going to be fun."

Em spun around, then ran toward the kitchen nearly knocking Nicole down as she stepped into the living area. "Whoa, little girl. Someone can get hurt."

"Mama, Mr. Slade's here and he said he doesn't want to miss a minute of our day."

Nicole looked up with a smile that nearly floored him. She had her hair pulled back with a baseball cap and she wore knee shorts and a white buttoned top. She was gorgeous. How could the excitement from one little girl and a smile from her mom turn his insides into mush?

Slade managed to give her a thumb's up.

"We're just about ready. I want to take a small backpack with a few essentials. Em, come with me."

"I'll sit right here if that's okay." He watched her take Em's hand and lead her through the hallway toward her room.

Slade walked around the small living area instead of sitting as he had said he would. Everything in her room was spotless and in its place. He stopped next to the sofa table where she had several pictures of Em and her dad and of Nicole and Tony. Slade couldn't help himself. He picked up the picture and stared at the happy couple. Nicole's smile was gorgeous as she looked at Tony. It was easy to see how much in love they'd been.

Instead of feeling a little jealous of the two of them, the picture saddened him. How had Nicole continued to be a mother in a town with no family after Tony was gone? How does someone deal with the death of a loved one?

And how did that man in the car fit into her life?

"We're ready." Nicole stepped into the living area carrying a small backpack.

Slade looked up from the picture. "I see where Em gets her good looks. You were a stunning couple."

Nicole nodded. "Thank you."

"And her dark features. They are definitely Tony's."

"You're right there. My entire family has blue or green eyes and blondish hair. I've been asked if I adopted her."

"That's not a very sensitive thing to say." Slade put the picture down not wanting his nosiness to ruin their afternoon. "I'm ready if my two girls are."

"Yes!" said Em as loud as she could.

Slade and Nicole both laughed.

"Then we'd better get going." He held open the door and Nicole and Em followed him to his car parked in the driveway.

As they passed Miss Tillie's, Slade slowed down and lowered the window. "Are you sure you don't want to go with us?"

"Thank you, but no. I'll see you in a few hours."

Slade headed toward the bridge to cross Biloxi Bay. "Are you still okay with taking Em to the children's museum?"

"Yes. Definitely."

"We're going to the museum?" Em shouted from the back seat. "I love that museum. I can do all that stuff really good, can't I, Mommie?"

"You certainly can."

All the way across the bridge and onto front beach, Em regaled them with stories of her past visits there until Slade pulled under a huge oak tree in the parking lot of the museum.

"Here we are, ladies. Let's see if we can find some wonderful things to do here." Slade helped both of them out of the car."

Em held onto Nicole's hand as she nearly dragged her mother into the doors of the museum. Slade bought tickets as the girls headed to the first display.

Slade followed close behind. Em stopped at a train depot display where she dressed as the engineer. From there she ran to The Port and pretended to put a shrimp net into the water to drag for shrimp. At each interactive station Em dressed in clothing from different periods in history and from different occupations. He loved watching her model the clothes and play the part of whatever she was wearing.

When she got to the Colossal Climbing Structure that reached all the way to the ceiling, she turned to Slade. "I can't climb that but one day I'll be able to."

Slade's heart went out to her. "Yes, one day you'll be able to climb all the way to the ceiling."

Without an argument, Em went to the next display.

Slade placed his hand on Nicole's elbow. He really wanted to hold her hand, but held back. Nicole had given no indication she wanted to be more than friends with him, and even though he was definitely attracted to her, he knew there was no room in his life for a family, not that he'd even know how to be a father and a husband.

No way would he make someone like Nicole unhappy as his dad had made his wife.

No, the Larson men didn't have a husband-like bone in their bodies.

Throughout the afternoon Slade watched Nicole interact with her daughter. He was amazed at the patience she showed even when Em didn't want to leave an exhibit or wanted to touch something that was prohibited.

It was hard to keep himself from thinking about being in that kind of position, but no matter how much he tried to see himself being a kind, patient father, he knew it would never happen. He was a workaholic, married to his work. He was afraid a child and a wife in his life would not make a difference.

He pulled his gaze away from Nicole and Em and watched several small groups gathering around the displays. It was easier to watch the others then to let himself imagine having a family.

No, he'd settle for borrowing a family now and then rather than making everyone miserable.

"Come with us, Mr. Slade." Em ran up to him and grabbed his hand.

Slade looked down at Em's small hand in his. Her innocent gesture was weaving its way into his heart. He swallowed before answering. "You lead the way."

At the next exhibit, Slade stood close to Nicole while Em and another little girl played.

"She's a great little girl. You've done a wonderful job with her. She's so inquisitive."

"I can't take all the credit. All six year olds are inquisitive. Their minds are like sponges soaking up anything and everything around them."

"You cut yourself short, Nicole. I've seen you around her. You're always teaching and molding her. Not all mothers and fathers know how to do that."

"As I said, she's typical in wanting to learn. I'm lucky she listens to me. Sometimes I try to figure out what Tony would've done in some of our situations, but that's not easy to do. I just give it a shot on my own or go down to Miss Tillie's. She always has the right answers for me."

Slade nodded. "I could've used a Miss Tillie in my life. Neither my mother nor my dad did the parenting thing very well. Everyone could use a Miss Tillie." He chuckled.

"Mom, come see." Em turned and motioned for

them to come closer.

They stepped near Em and listened to her give him her elementary and simplified version of the next display.

By the time Em led Nicole and Slade through most of the entire museum, Nicole found a place for them to sit. She felt Em's forehead. "Are you feeling okay, Em?"

Em squeezed next to Nicole and placed her head against Nicole's arm. "I'm tired."

Slade left to get them a drink. When he returned, it was easy to see Em wasn't her normal bubbly self. "She okay?" he whispered.

"Just a little tired." Nicole turned to Em, who had closed her eyes. "Em, Mr. Slade brought you something to drink. Can you sit up?"

Em raised her head. She took the drink without saying anything and sipped on it.

"Maybe the beach will have to wait for another day," Nicole said.

"That's perfectly okay," he agreed. "It's not going anywhere and there's a sunset every evening." He sat next to Em and watched her take a few swallows. His chest tightened. Remembering how she had to have a transfusion a few weeks ago, he wasn't sure exactly what to do. It was obvious the little girl wasn't up to doing anything else today.

"Did you like the stuff in the museum, Mr. Slade?"

"Yep. This is a great place, but it might be time to get us home. I'm a little tired. Is that okay with you?"

She nodded. "I'm tired too."

He took her hand and she walked next to him. By the time they got to the parking lot, Slade reached down and picked her up. She laid her head against his shoulder.

Nicole mouthed a thank you.

Instead of stopping at Miss Tillie's, Slade drove straight to Nicole's. After helping Nicole get Em settled in her bedroom, they headed to the porch.

Nicole set up her monitor on a small table then took a seat in one of her rockers. Slade sat on the swing.

"I'm sorry about our night," she said, "but I couldn't enjoy myself worrying that maybe she's this tired because she's about to have another episode. I've already called Miss Tillie."

"You don't have to apologize to me. I understand. We don't have to go anywhere, but if it's okay, I'd love to hang around a little. I'll order something for us to eat and we can enjoy your front porch."

"You'd want to do that?"

"Why wouldn't I? I eat in restaurants all the time. This would be a treat."

"I'd like that as well."

Nicole stared out into the street and Slade wondered if she actually saw anything.

"I don't know how you do everything you do," he said hoping he wasn't intruding and getting too personal. "My life is so easy compared with yours."

"We all have our problems."

Nicole looked at him. Her face was serious and Slade longed to see a smile on her face.

"Mine happens to be a sick daughter," Nicole continued. "She's my life so I don't regret anything I do for her. I wish things were different though. It breaks my heart knowing she's not well and can't do everything other little girls do."

"You're amazing, Nicole Russo." He pushed the swing and closed his eyes for a second. "This is wonderful. So peaceful. I'm glad we're not at a busy restaurant."

"I like this too, but are you sure you don't want me to fix us something to eat?"

"Nope. I'll call in something from anywhere you'd like. Your night out isn't going to be spent cooking."

The Yellow Rooster was still open so he drove the short distance to pick up fish tacos for him and Nicole and a hot dog and fries for Em.

When he returned with The Yellow Rooster's take-out bag, Nicole grinned. "I see you went to my competition."

Slade forced a smile. "Closest place opened. I like the taco. How about you?"

"I do too," she said. "Gary might be competition, but I like the guy, and the food is good. I go over there sometimes, too."

Slade almost thanked her for supporting his business, but stopped before he told her he owned the restaurant. Tonight wasn't the night. He was enjoying her company too much to ruin the evening.

After they ate, Em went back to her room to play with her iPad.

"Is it okay if we go back out on the porch? Will she know to call us if she needs something?" Slade asked as he helped Nicole clean the table.

"Yes. I'll go remind her where we'll be, and I'll take the monitor."

~

Nicole stood next to Em's bed for a few extra minutes before turning on her night light. She prayed her daughter wasn't near another episode, then pulling in a deep breath, she headed to the porch.

"Em's already asleep. I think she'll be okay."

Slade patted the swing for her to sit. She didn't let herself think as she slid onto the swing next to him and relaxed.

"Does she always get this exhausted when she does something like this afternoon?" he asked as he stretched his arm across the back of her shoulders.

She rested against his arm and closed her eyes letting the feeling of protection sweep over her. She didn't want to rely on anyone, especially someone like Slade who wasn't going to be around for very long, but she didn't let that thought take away the enjoyment of being near him.

"Unfortunately, yes, especially recently. She wants to do everything she used to do, but she can't. I'm so scared she won't be able to stay in school. She's so excited about being in first grade. I hope she can handle it."

Slade pulled her a little closer to him. She relaxed against his shoulder.

"That would be awful," he said.

"It would. She loves her teacher and the children in her class. Every day I think she'll feel better and stronger, but I guess I need to be a realist. It's not going to happen on its own."

"I'm glad she was able to have a little fun today. I loved watching her." He chuckled. "I guess you can tell I haven't been around kids much."

She looked at him. "I think you do just fine with her. She loves you and Mac."

"I guess it's hard for her not to have a father figure

in her life. Does she talk about her dad?"

"Not really. She knows she had a daddy and loves looking at the pictures I have of her with him, but she doesn't remember much about him. I try hard to keep his memories alive, but sometimes I think she only remembers what I've told her about him."

"That's sad, but I'm sure in her heart she knows he loved her. That feeling will be with her always."

"See," Nicole said as she looked up into his eyes, "you talk as if you've been around children all your life."

"Thank you. I'll take that as a compliment because as I told you, I haven't."

Nicole leaned against the swing with the weight of Slade's arm still on her shoulders. "This is nice. Thank you for staying."

"My pleasure." Slade turned his body slightly and pulled her close to him.

She knew he was going to kiss her and for a second, she panicked. Did she dare allow him? Should she pull away? Should she explain that she hadn't kissed anyone since Tony had died? That kissing him would complicate things since he wasn't staying on the coast?

She did none of those things. She looked up. He was smiling.

"I want to kiss you, but you look as if I'm about to attack you."

The way he said the words and the way his lip tilted up at the corners made her relax.

"I think I want to kiss you as well." She surprised herself by lifting her face toward him.

He didn't disappoint. He lowered his face and touched his lips to hers. They were firm and warm. The kiss took her breath away. For a few moments she forgot she was a single mom with a sick child and debts she had no idea how to handle. Instead she relished Slade's body next to hers and the warmth that spread through her entire being.

She didn't want the kiss to end, but it did.

Slade eased away from her with a smile on his face, pulled her close to him again, but didn't say anything.

She rested her head against his chest and closed her eyes. "It's easy to forget how nice it is to have a man hold you."

"I'm sorry you lost Tony," he said. "I want you to know I appreciate your letting me step in and spend a little time with you and Emily."

"I've never let another man do that."

Slade sat up straighter and looked into her eyes. "Then I really do feel special about our time together, even if it's for the little time I'm here."

Nicole eased her head back down against him.

Maybe that's why I'm letting you do this. I know you won't try to step into Tony's shoes.

But even as those thoughts materialized, she felt a tiny ache in her heart. Slade Larson wasn't the man she thought he was when she'd first met him, and with each time she spent with him she knew she would like their time together to be a little longer.

But that would never happen. His home and life were in New York.

He looked down at her. "Penny for your thoughts."

"Those thoughts aren't worth even a penny."

He laughed. "Still I'd like to know what you think about me being here on this swing with you."

"I think you've made me remember it's okay to let

myself have a little fun, and for that I really do thank you."

"And the kiss?" He asked and smiled big.

She dropped her gaze then looked back up to him. "That was nice too."

He sat up with a grin that took her breath away.

"Just nice? Man, I must be out of practice."

She pulled away, playfully punched him on the arm, then laughed. "Maybe a little nicer than nice. It was wonderful."

Slade got serious. "I'm glad you feel that way. I thought it was wonderful as well. I've wanted to do that since we first met, but I was afraid you would've punched me."

"Maybe at first I would've, but not now. Slade, I haven't kissed anyone since . . ."

Slade pulled Nicole to him. "I know. You don't have to explain. I'm just glad you let your guard down with me."

With those words, she leaned into him, snuggled closer and kissed him again. She never thought she'd ever be bold enough to do something like that, but it was easy with Slade. He had a way of making her feel as if she'd been with him all of her life.

She was conscious of Slade's body and ran her hand from behind his neck down his chest and ended at his side.

He pulled away slightly and looked at her. "I like the feel of your hand on me."

She bit her lip. "I couldn't control myself. I had to do that."

He chuckled and pulled her close to him again. With her head snuggled against his neck, he rubbed her back. "And I like the feel of your entire body against me. I'm so glad we didn't get to the restaurant tonight. This is definitely much better."

"Mama."

Nicole pulled away. "That's the monitor. Em's awake."

"Go on. I'm fine right here."

Nicole rushed into the house to Em's room, waiting for the guilt of being with Slade swoop down on her.

It didn't come. For once she had allowed herself to enjoy herself and she didn't feel guilty one bit. She stepped into Em's room, went to her bed and hugged her daughter. She'd do anything for Em, but maybe she was learning to let herself do what she had to do and still actually have a life.

Even if Slade Larson left tomorrow to go to New York to his other life, she'd always be grateful to him for opening her eyes to live again.

Of course, having Slade here for as long as possible wouldn't be so bad either

Chapter Nine

For the next several days Nicole racked her brain trying to find some way to come up with enough money to pay the money she owed to Barry Keats. The only thing feasible was another loan from the bank. It wasn't something she wanted to do, but at least the bank wouldn't demand large lump payments. She visited the local branch where she had a small nest egg to help cover Em's future medical expenses and filled out the needed paper work. She was told to give the bank forty-eight hours.

Two days later she walked into the bank eager to get her money to be able to pay Mr. Keats. It only took a couple of minutes before she walked out of the bank with a heavy heart. The committee had turned her down for a loan. She knew she wasn't a good risk, but she never imagined they'd flat refuse her.

She plopped down on a bench outside the bank. Now what?

Barry Keats couldn't be ignored. She had to come

up with some money to offer him against the loan, because as he'd reminded her, the interest rate was compounding the money she owed.

What had Tony been thinking?

She looked around the small Marsh Isles business district. A few people walked along the sidewalk but most simply drove by in their cars oblivious to what she faced if she couldn't pay off Tony's debt. Her situation seemed hopeless, but Nicole wasn't giving up. She wasn't sure what her next move would be, but there had to be something she could do. Those were her thoughts as she climbed in her Jeep and headed home.

I won't give up. I can find a way.

Miss Tillie stood at the stove as Nicole went into the house. "Hey, Miss Tilllie. Where's Em?"

"She's in her room playing dolls." Miss Tillie crossed her arms. "Why are you home? What's wrong?"

Nicole sat down at her kitchen table.

Miss Tillie pulled out a chair and sat down and took Nicole's hand. "Please tell me what's wrong."

Nicole shook her head. "I don't want you to worry."

"Oh, pshaw, if you can't share a problem with a friend who can you tell?"

Nicole smiled. "You're right. I thought I could handle the problem alone. Now I'm not so sure."

Miss Tillie sat up straight. "I'm all ears."

Nicole took a deep breath and opened up about Tony making the loan. When she finished, she looked up. "Now I'm at my wit's end. He insinuated he'd take my Jeep and this house, but, of course, I couldn't give him this house if I wanted to, but he could go after my café."

"Oh, Nicole. I'm so sorry. Let me help. I have money."

"No, absolutely not. I would never take your money."

Miss Tillie shook her head. "Why? Why would you refuse an old lady the privilege of helping someone she loves?" She took Nicole's hand. "I have only one daughter and one granddaughter. They've been taken care of in a trust fund, but I have money I could give to you. I don't know how much you owe the man but I could help."

"No, I could never let you do that."

"You think about it. You can call it a loan if you want. Wouldn't you rather owe me money than that man? I don't know him, but I don't trust him."

"I don't trust him either." Nicole stood up, walked around the table and hugged Miss Tillie. "I'll consider your offer especially if I need the money to help Em get better treatment."

"And when that time comes don't you dare allow money problems to stand in your way. That little girl deserves the best care possible."

"Thank you. I don't want to be indebted to anyone, especially you, but I'll do anything to keep Em healthy. Dr. Murry keeps assuring me she's okay for the moment." She hugged Miss Tillie.

After Miss Tillie left, Nicole tapped on Em's door.

"Mama, come see. Henrietta and Miss Lucy are drinking tea with me. You want some?"

"Certainly." Nicole sat down in one of Em's tiny chairs and played teatime with Em and her favorite dolls, all the while looking at her daughter and wondering how she and Em would be able to survive if she had to sell everything to pay off Mr. Keats.

Getting a loan from Miss Tillie might hold him off while she worked to save more.

Maybe things were looking up. Still, she wouldn't stop looking for other ways to get the money to pay off her debts.

~

Slade walked into the Marsh Isles Police Department and asked to see William Mason, Miss Tillie's nephew.

After the receptionist made a call, he was led down a hallway.

"He's waiting for you," the young officer said.

With a knock, Slade opened the door. Mr. Mason stood up then walked around his desk. He stuck out his hand and shook with a firm hold. "My officer told me you're Mac's brother."

"Sure am. I'm on the coast helping him out for a few weeks."

Slade figured the guy was at least six feet tall because he stood eye-to-eye with him and was probably about the same age as he was. "Miss Tillie gave me your name. She said you were a patrol officer, but obviously you're not."

William shook Slade's hand. "I love my Aunt Tillie. Who wouldn't?" He laughed. "I simply don't try to correct her anymore. I haven't been a patrol officer in years. I made detective a few years ago."

"Quite impressive."

William walked around the desk, sat down and stretched his legs. He laughed. "My aunt still thinks I'm the little brat who used to play behind her house. I'm surprised she remembered I'm with the department here, but like I said, I love her dearly." The man straightened up and got serious. "I guess you're here about the man you asked about."

"I am. I'm not even sure if you can do anything for me, but I thought I'd give it a try."

"I'm glad you did. I have someone looking into it right now. We were overloaded here when you called, but I'll have something for you today. If he has a record it'll show up, but if he doesn't, I'm not sure what we can do."

"I understand and knew that before I came. Until we figure out what part he's playing in Nicole's life, we can only keep an eye on him."

"And we can certainly do that. I know Nicole. I've seen her quite a few times at Aunt Tillie's house. She's a sweet lady and a good mother and she's doing a good job of keeping life stable for her little girl since her husband died."

"That she is. That's why I'm so concerned about this guy. It might be nothing, but my gut tells me not to turn my head."

"I have learned to listen to my gut, but even more to listen to my aunt. If she's worried about something, I don't turn my head either." He picked up the phone. "Let me give her a call and see what she thinks about all this."

Slade watched him closely. He was usually good at first impressions and his first impression of William was someone he'd like. He reminded Slade of some of his business associates who were dedicated to their jobs.

William hung up his phone. "No answer. I'll try to get her a little later." He got up. "I'll get in touch with you as soon as we find something out about that tag and do a little digging on that guy."

Slade walked out of the police department feeling a little better knowing someone was looking into the man's past. He got in his car to return to Slade's, but instead turned down a side street and found a parking place near to Miss Tillie's.

"How're doing?" He opened the picket fence gate and walked up to the porch.

"I'm doing great. Come up and I'll get you a glass of tea."

"No, ma'am. I really don't have time. I wanted to talk to you for a moment." He sat on the top step. He explained what he'd talked about in his meeting with her nephew. "He called you but didn't get an answer. We wanted to ask you a few questions about Nicole and that man. I took a chance you'd be here though."

Miss Tillie looked around. "I guess I left my phone inside and didn't hear it. I'll tell you what I know. In fact, today Nicole let me in on why she's been so upset."

Slade listened while Miss Tillie told him about Barry and the loan and now the money Nicole owed.

"Slade, I offered to give her the money or even lend it to her, but she's such a stubborn, proud girl, she wouldn't take it."

"Which means if I offered to help, she'd throw me out of the house."

"Yes, but the girl is making herself sick worrying about this. I really want us to help her."

"We'll figure something out." Slade shook his head. "I can't believe her husband borrowed money from someone like that man. Now it all makes sense." He stood up. "Now that we know his connection to her, I'll talk with your nephew again and see what we can do legally."

"Thank you, Slade. I hate to see our Nicole so worried."

"I am as well, but we can deal with this low-life." He waved and headed to his car. He hadn't missed Miss Tillie's words when she called Nicole "our Nicole." He liked the sound of that. With a quick look down the block to Nicole's house, he headed to his car, but it took all his willpower not to go to her and assure her things would be okay.

Before he talked with her or confronted Mr. Keats, he had to come up with a plan of action.

~

Two days later Slade leaned against his car on Paradise Lane, just a block away from The Yellow Rooster. With William's help, Slade located Barry Keats and surprisingly the man had agreed to meet him.

He pulled out his phone and looked at the time. Deciding he'd wait a few more minutes he looked out over the calm water of the bay. The winds were calm this evening causing only a few small ripples on the water. At that moment he wished he'd be here enjoying the view with Nicole instead of waiting for the man who had given her husband a loan.

He wondered if Nicole ever walked along the bay road simply to enjoy the view. If she didn't hate him for doing what he was about to do, maybe he could actually help her enjoy life. In spite of knowing he wouldn't be on the coast for long, he still wanted to spend more time with her. Sitting with her the other night on her porch simply reinforced that feeling and made him wonder if a real home life could one day be in his future.

He shook his head. Where was all that coming from? Thinking about a home life with anyone was ridiculous. Where was the sane businessman who never let himself get emotional about anything? Was he losing it?

"Maybe I am." He laughed and turned to leave.

Just as he pushed himself away from his car, a grey sedan pulled up behind him, the same one that had passed Nicole's house. A middle-aged man stepped out of the car. His grey dress pants and button-up white shirt impressed Slade, but the smirk on his face sent Slade's blood pressure up, knowing he probably intimidated people like Nicole with that look.

But Slade wasn't easily intimidated. He walked right up to him and stuck out his hand. "Mr. Keats, thank you for coming."

Barry Keats reciprocated with a limp shake. "If someone tells me I might get reimbursed for a loan, I'll show up with bells on. Now what is it you're proposing?"

"Did you bring a copy of the contract Tony Russo signed when you gave him the money?"

Barry reached in the front seat of his car and pulled out a piece of paper. "This is only a copy, but you can see Tony's signature. You can take it. Check it out with someone to make sure it's his if you'd like, then we can talk. The terms are all here. The amount he borrowed and the interest. I tried to make it easy for you. I figured out to the penny what Mrs. Russo owes me."

Again reining in his temper, Slade took the paper. "Thank you for bringing it. How about we meet tomorrow morning? I'll go over this contract and we'll see if we can come up with an agreement. Is nine okay?"

"Sounds good to me." Barry started to walk away, but turned back. "Who are you to Nicole?"

"Just a friend who admires her for all she's doing for herself and her little girl."

The smirk again crossed his face. "She might be a hard worker but she must be pretty stupid to let a husband get her in such a bind."

Slade took two big steps nearer to the guy, but gritted his teeth and pulled in his anger. Slapping this guy around would get him nowhere and might make Keats decide not to go through with the deal. He stopped and said nothing.

Barry raised a hand. "See you tomorrow."

Slade watched him drive away, said a few choice words under his breath, then got in the car. Instead of driving back to Slade's or his hotel he headed to the police station to talk with William once more.

At nine o'clock the next morning Slade pulled up behind Barry's sedan. He wasn't sure about the results of this meeting, but having him here early was a good sign.

"Thanks for meeting me early." Slade pulled out an envelope. "These are the terms I'd like you to look over. I will give you a lump sum to take care of the entire loan, but your interest rates are not in line with today's market." He chose his words carefully so Barry wouldn't walk away.

"But those interest rates are what Mr. Russo agreed to. The man was desperate."

"I understand that, but we're both businessmen." Slade struggled not to choke from calling him a legitimate name. "We both know terms can be changed if both parties agree. Mrs. Russo can't pay these fees and if I take care of the loan, I simply won't pay them."

"Then we don't have a deal, do we?" Barry stuck out the paper for Slade to take back.

"I think you need to look at what I'm offering. You'll get your money back plus a sensible interest. I think it's a good deal." What he wanted to say was no one in his right mind would agree to the exorbitant interest rates Barry had charged, but he said nothing else since Tony definitely had taken them.

Barry frowned and pulled back the paper. "I know my legal rights. I have the man's signature."

"Yes, you do, but I'm wondering if the IRS will agree with you or if you even notify them of your profits from people like Mrs. Russo."

Barry squirmed then threw his shoulders back in a show of bravado. "Are you threatening me?"

"Call it what you want. Let's say it's the same thing you did to Mrs. Russo by threatening to take her Jeep. I simply like my associates to know exactly what's available for me if we can't come to terms. I'm not trying to rip you off. Tony Russo made a bad business call and got stuck in a financial muck, but I don't see why we have to drag his widow through it as well."

Barry dropped his arms by his side still clutching the envelope.

"My phone number is on the paper." Slade continued hoping to end this meeting soon. The sooner he left this lowlife, the happier he'd be. "Read the terms closely and you'll see it's a pretty good deal for you. Call me this evening and I can get the money to you via a cashier's check by next week. If a check doesn't work for you, we can make other arrangements. I'll be stuck up in New York for a while so I've arranged a representative from here to bring the paperwork and the money to you. You agree to the terms, sign the papers and you'll get your loan paid off."

Slade stuck out his hand again and hoped the man would reciprocate. It went against every bone in his body doing business with someone like him, but he knew Tony's obligation had to be dealt with and Nicole certainly didn't have the resources to pay it off.

"That woman must be a good lay for you to do this for her." Barry laughed.

Slade stepped back and clenched his fists.

"Good day, Mr. Keats. I hope to hear from you soon."

He turned and walked away from the man before he did something he'd regret.

~

Slade stared out his office window at the New York skyline. He'd always loved the beauty and energy of the city, but today the only thing he saw was traffic and chaos below him. He'd been back in the city for three days trying to stay busy not to think about what he'd left behind in Marsh Isles.

With a quick knock, Kelli walked in. "I arranged to have the cashier's check ready by two this afternoon. Is that a good time for you?"

Slade turned away from the scene below and pulled out his desk chair. "Yes. I'll eat a late lunch and stop by the bank on my way back. Thanks." Slade concentrated on his computer screen hoping Kelli wouldn't ask any questions.

"Since you didn't give me any details about what

this money is for and who Barry Keats is, I'm at a loss as to what to put in the books. In fact I haven't even typed up any paperwork to finalize this. This isn't for anything illegal, is it?"

Slade rolled his desk chair back, stretched, then laughed. "Do you really have to ask a question like that? Of course it's all legal. Just put it down as repayment for a personal loan."

"A personal loan. For you? I don't understand. When did you borrow this?"

"You're not going to let it go, are you?"

"Nope." She sat down and crossed her arms. "I'm pretty caught up with my work. I can sit here forever."

"If you have to know, a lady I went to high school with in Marsh Isles got stuck in a bad situation concerning a loan her late husband made. I'm paying off the loan."

"You're paying off the loan? I haven't drawn up any papers with the terms of her repayment. Shouldn't I do that before you pay the loan off?"

"Let's say I'll get around to that later if that's what I decide to do."

"What? This isn't like you. You don't do anything that's not by the books."

"Kelli, this is a personal matter. Can we leave it at that?"

She shook her head. "You're the boss." Getting up, she walked to the door, then turned back to Slade. "Don't get yourself in any trouble, especially if it's with a woman."

"I appreciate your concern, but I can guarantee you this is all above board."

Kelli smiled and left Slade sitting alone. He knew

everything he was doing was legal. He just wished he could say it was okay with Nicole. When she found out he'd gone behind her back, he was going to be in hot water. No way would she agree to his paying off the loan, but Slade knew he couldn't stand by and do nothing. Nicole needed her money to take care of her daughter, and he certainly didn't want Miss Tillie to go into her savings.

He felt good about what he was doing, and he knew Miss Tillie and Detective Mason were all on board with it.

One day he hoped Nicole would be as well.

He rolled his chair back to his desk and finished the wording on the paperwork he was sending to his representative in Marsh Isles. It was the same attorney he'd used when he'd bought The Yellow Rooster from Nicole.

He reread what he'd already written, making sure he was careful how he'd worded the contract because before he got his money, Barry had to agree to leave Nicole alone. Any harassment on his part would result in Slade contacting the law.

He worked on the document, changing it several times before he was satisfied with the wording. He had to be sure Nicole and Em would be safe.

Chapter Ten

With Slade in New York and Em in school, Nicole devoted most of her days to the café working hard to save money for Christmas and to have some to pay Mr. Keats. It had been weeks since she'd heard from him, but she didn't dare reach out to him since she didn't have the amount of money he was demanding. If he called before Christmas, she had already decided to ask Miss Tillie for a loan. She hoped it wouldn't have to happen.

Slade flew to the coast on Thanksgiving morning where she, Em, Miss Tillie and Mac met him. They went straight to a fine dining restaurant for a late meal. Afterwards, Mac went to the restaurant and Slade took Em and Nicole to find a Christmas tree.

By Friday evening, the tree was up and decorated. Nicole picked up the last box and put it away in the attic, then pulled out the broom and dustpan. She walked back into the living room and stopped. Slade sat on the floor with Em next to the tree. Em had her hand on one of the ornaments she'd hung there a few minutes before but she was again telling him the story behind the shiny pink unicorn that her daddy had given her. It was a story that Nicole told her every Christmas, but she was sure Em didn't actually remember receiving the ornament.

Nicole stepped into the room. "Em, are you ready to go to Miss Tillie's?"

"Yes, ma'am. I have Miss Lucy and Miss Henrietta and my pajamas. That's all I need, except for my iPad and I can carry that."

"Then it looks like you're all ready to go. We'll walk you there as soon as I finish in here." She swept up a few more needles.

Em jumped up and ran to her room.

Slade pulled himself up and brushed off his shorts. For late November the weather was still extremely warm, and Nicole couldn't keep looking at his long muscular legs. She'd missed him so much while he was gone, she couldn't wait to have some alone time with him when they went out to eat.

"Our reservations are for six," Slade said. "I'll be back in about an hour to get you. Casual will be fine."

"Are you sure? I don't want to be underdressed."

"This is the coast, remember? See you in about an hour."

Nicole knew it wouldn't take her an hour to get ready, but she was excited to be with Slade tonight so she found herself hurrying. She loved putting up the tree, but now it was time to be with Slade.

~

At five-thirty Slade and Nicole walked out of Miss Tillie's house. Both of them turned and waved to Em who was already sitting in Miss Tillie's lap in front of the television. As soon as Nicole stepped on the porch, she hesitated. As much as she wanted to be alone with Slade, the all-too-familiar feeling of guilt about leaving Em settled over her.

As if Slade understood, he put his arm around her shoulder and pulled her close to him. "You're a good mother, Nicole. I don't want you to feel guilty about leaving her, but I swear we'll be just a few minutes from here."

"I know. I'm being silly. I leave her all the time with Miss Tillie. She knows to call me if Em shows any signs of an episode."

"Of course she will, and I have to say Em looked great today. She really had fun putting up that tree."

They walked down the steps and out to the street. "She did, didn't she? I'm glad you were able to be there with us. It meant the world to her."

"I wouldn't have missed it." He opened the car door for her. "But now it's time to have some grown-up time."

It didn't take long for Slade to cross the bridge and then ride down the beach where he pulled into the parking lot of one of the newer hotels on the front beach in Biloxi. The grounds were lush with huge tropical trees, manicured lawns and blooming bougainvillea bushes. She felt as if she were driving into a tropical palace. "Is this where you're staying?"

"It is and there's a great restaurant I'd like to take you to unless you have a preference for someplace else."

"No, no preference. This is fine. I've never been in this hotel, uh restaurant," she corrected herself, "but

I've heard they're very good."

And expensive. And I probably need my head examined going into a hotel now with Slade.

"The restaurant is excellent. I think you won't be disappointed," he said, giving her one of his devastating smiles.

Immediately she relaxed, but not entirely, not with the tingling sensations caused from just being with him.

She swallowed as he walked around the car, reassuring herself that dinner with a man was okay. Nothing else would happen. But, even convincing herself she was not doing a bad thing, guilt set in. She should be worrying about Em, not going into a hotel with Slade.

He opened the door for her, and as she slid out, he pulled her into his arms. She leaned into him, closed her eyes and let him hold her.

"I know you're feeling guilty about leaving Em," he said. "If you don't want to stay we'll go back."

Reluctantly she stepped away and looked up into his eyes.

Could he possibly understand how she felt? He wasn't a father. He wasn't responsible for a sick child even though as he said, Em looked good today.

He still kept his hands on her arms. "We can eat another time if you'd rather or we can stop and pick something up."

She smiled. How could she tell him no? He was doing everything in his power to make her feel good. "No, I'm being a little paranoid and I don't even know why. She didn't even look tired when we left her. I want to be here and have a nice grown-up dinner, and I want to spend a little time with you. Maybe it's what I need."

He let out a big breath and smiled. "I'm sure it is. Everyone needs a little me-time."

"Anyway, I'm starving."

"That's the Nicole I know." He led her into the hotel lobby then to the elevator.

On the eleventh floor, they stepped out of the elevator into a huge glassed restaurant. Nicole realized this wasn't the run-of-the-mill tourist eateries. "Wow, this is really nice," she whispered, then looked down at her simple sundress she'd worn.

"Yep, it is."

"I feel a little, no, a lot underdressed. Are you sure we can go in like this?"

Before he could answer, a hostess met them. "Good evening, Mr. Larson. We have your table ready." The elegantly dressed lady led them to a window table, set off from the rest of the tables by a row of tropical plants. "Is this okay?" she asked.

"Certainly," he said, then pulled out a chair for Nicole.

"I'm impressed."

"Yes, I lucked up when my magician secretary found this hotel for me. She said she picked it because of this restaurant."

Another well-dressed lady walked up and handed them a menu. "Can I get the two of you something to drink?"

Both of them ordered wine, then Nicole leaned back against a beautifully upholstered chair and took in the blues and greens of the water, sailboats waiting to enjoy the sunset, and birds gliding by. "This is so beautiful. Most of the time I'm so busy I don't see the water for days."

"We all need to stop and take the time to see what's around us. I do the same thing in New York. I never hit the tourist sites, and if I'm near Times Square or the Empire State Building, I'm surprised at the awesomeness that's around me. You're not alone in taking your surroundings for granted. Of course, being here is really special."

"I agree." She stared at the view out the window and let the weight of the world slide off her shoulders. Even though she could have worn something dressier, she felt beautiful sitting in this luxury.

Many of the men in the restaurant wore suits or sports coats, but not Slade. He looked so cool and totally at ease in this fancy surroundings, reminding Nicole once more how their two worlds were so different. Still she was determined to enjoy this evening. Knowing how her life was going, this might be the one and only time she'd ever find herself here, especially with someone as handsome as Slade.

"Since the hostess had your table waiting, I have a feeling you knew I'd agree to come with you here this evening."

Slade grinned. "You can't blame a man for hoping. But you're right, I did reserve the table. I talked with Miss Tillie earlier and she agreed to watch Em even before you called her today. She and I both feel as though you need some time to enjoy life a little."

"Gosh, I didn't know I looked so pitiful."

He squeezed her hand. "Not pitiful by any means. Just a hard working single mother who needs to remember it's okay to have a little fun once in a while."

"Thank you. This really is nice. I'm thoroughly

impressed and glad we came."

~

After ordering lobster for both of them, Slade sipped his wine. He watched Nicole and hoped she'd feel comfortable enough to enjoy the evening. If she only knew how beautiful she was, she'd understand she fit into this elegant room no matter what she wore. She'd pulled her hair back for their day of decorating the tree, but tonight it hung loose around her face highlighting her smooth skin and big blue eyes.

But it was her lips that made him swallow. After having tasted them, he couldn't stop thinking about feeling them again.

He lifted his wine glass to have something else to think about.

"So how long will you be on the coast this time?" Her question brought him back to reality.

"Not sure. I'm still working with Mac and his books. He's done a lot of improvements since I've been gone, and I think there's light at the end of the tunnel. At least I hope there is."

"That's good. That restaurant is Mac's life. I'd hate to see him lose it."

"I know, and I'd love to keep it in the family."

"How about your job in New York? Did you get a lot of work done while you were home?"

"I did. Kelli worked me to death. Sometimes I think she runs that office and I work for her."

"But you would never tell her that, right?"

"She knows."

"I hope you can stay for a little while. I missed not having you around."

Her words sent a steak of heat through his body. He

hoped his voice sounded cooler than he was. "Yep. I missed being here. I was enjoying my time spent with Mac. It's been years since we've been able to do that." He took a drink to settle his body down. "And being with you and Em was special. Very special."

Her smile told him she felt the same.

"Tell me what you do in your spare time in New York."

He thought a moment before answering. What did he do? "That's a hard question."

Nicole laughed. "No, it's a simple question. What do you do with yourself when you're not in your office?"

"I really don't do much. I guess I'm a workaholic. I like being in my office. It's comfortable and has a gorgeous view of the city. I'm usually the last one to leave my building. On nice evenings, I walk home. There are several small pubs and restaurants within the few blocks to my condo. I stop there sometimes. Sometimes I pick up food and eat in the condo."

"That sounds nice. I've never lived in a big city and had everything within walking distance. That would be nice. What about weekends? Do you take in plays?"

"Sometimes. I used to do that more when I first got to the city. I still do if there's a new play I think I'd enjoy or if I have a date who wants to go."

"So I'm assuming you don't have anyone special up there waiting for you or we wouldn't be sitting here together."

Slade laughed. "No, no one special. I have a couple female friends who work in the building. There's nothing we have in common, except needing to get out once in a while. There're also a few guys who get together once a month, sometimes more, and if I can, I join them. They meet at a local sports bar. I like football, as you well know, and it's always more fun to watch a game with a bunch of rowdy men than alone in your own home."

"Since I've become an adult, I find I like football too. Tony never seemed to be too interested, or maybe he never had the time to devote to watching it, so it's been awhile since I've really enjoyed a good game."

"We're right in the middle of football season. Maybe we can catch a game on TV sometimes."

"That would be great."

The waitress brought their stuffed lobsters.

"This is gorgeous." Nicole's face lit up. "I think I'm starving."

"Good. Eat up."

After a few bites, Nicole turned the conversation back to him. "You were quite the football player in high school. I'm embarrassed to say I only went to one game. My friends and I weren't into sport, but it was hard not to know who the stars on the team were."

"I thought I was a star, but it didn't take long before I found out my talents were not that great. I didn't even get an offer to play at the smaller community colleges. Talk about a hurt ego."

"Were your parents still together then?"

"No, Mom had already moved on, and with the restaurant, Dad rarely was able to get to the games. Not that it mattered."

"Of course it matters. Parents need to support their children's interest. I didn't do much in high school. I studied and got all A's. I was member of the band and the choir, and whenever we put on a program, my mom was always there. Even if I was sitting on the back row on stage, I knew she was there watching. It mattered. Believe me."

"You were a lucky girl. I wish I would've gotten to know you when we were teenagers."

"No, we never would've clicked. We were very poor. Mom made all my clothes, but she was an excellent seamstress so I knew I looked as good as the other girls, but not always the trendiest."

"A seamstress. That's amazing. I'm not sure my mother even had a needle and thread to reattach a button. I remember one time I lost a button and she told me to just throw the shirt away. It was a favorite shirt. I had the button so I went to the store and bought a tiny sewing kit and fixed it myself."

"I'm impressed. Star football player and resourceful with a needle." Nicole picked up her glass of wine. "Seriously though. I'm sorry your parents weren't involved with your childhood. In that respect I guess I was the lucky one."

"And I'm the lucky one tonight. I'm glad you came with me."

Chapter Eleven

Nicole's body warmed at his words and quivered at the thoughts that zipped through her brain and her heart. Never in the time since Tony's death had she allowed herself to even think about being with another man, but tonight sitting with Slade made her remember what it was like to be a woman.

And tonight she knew she wanted to feel like a woman again.

But that could never be. Em was at Miss Tillie's. She couldn't expect her to keep her all evening. No matter how much she enjoyed being with Slade, she wanted to get home at a reasonable hour.

She ate her stuffed lobster in silence pushing away the guilt from wanting to spend as much time with Slade as possible.

Her phone vibrated bringing her out of her deep thoughts. She grabbed the phone from her purse afraid that Em needed her.

"Miss Tillie, is anything wrong?" she said before

even saying hello. Her heart beat against her chest expecting the familiar words that Em needed to go to the hospital.

Instead Miss Tillie eased her mind.

"Thank you. Are you sure? Ok. Good night. I love you."

Slade had put his fork down and stared at her. "Is everything okay?"

Nicole nodded. "Yes. I let my mind run wild when I saw it was Miss Tillie calling."

"But Em's okay?"

"Yes, in fact, Miss Tillie said she put her in bed with her and wanted her to spend the night. She's already asleep. I can pick her up in the morning."

He leaned back against his chair and let out a big breath. "Oh thank goodness. That's wonderful news."

Again Nicole nodded. "It is. I guess I live in panic mode these days." With shaking hands she lifted her wine glass. "I probably need a bottle of this," she said then laughed.

"You and me both." He reached across the table and took her hand. "If Em is spending the night with Miss Tillie, you can relax a little. I could tell you were in deep thought even before the phone call."

She took another swallow. If he only knew where she'd let her mind go, he'd realize just how deep her thoughts had gone. "You're right. I don't have to rush home, but I don't want to keep you from something you might need to do."

"Oh no. I'm off the clock tonight. I'm not going back to Slade's this evening. Even Mac agreed my job tonight was to make your night special."

"Thanks to both of you."

She finished eating her dinner and made small talk with Slade, but her mind refused to behave. Instead, every iota of her body yearned to be in Slade's arms. After the waitress took away their plates and poured them another glass of wine, Nicole sat up straight and spoke before she let herself think about what she was about to say.

"Slade, I'd like you to take me to your room."

For a moment, he stared at her and said nothing. Slowly he put his glass down. "You want to go to my room?"

Oh heavens, did I really ask that?

"I think so." She answered in a whisper.

Again he reached across the table and took her hand. "Nicole, there is nothing more I'd rather do than to take you to my room, but I'm not sure I'd be content to just show you the décor and the scenery. I'd want a lot more, and I'm not sure you're ready for that."

She swallowed. "I am."

"I'm not sure you are. You're vulnerable and scared and feeling alone. . ."

Before he had time to continue, she sat up straighter. "I'm all of those things, but it has taken me three years to feel comfortable enough with a man to ask. . . what I just asked." She chuckled low. "And as luck would have it, the man I've asked is trying to change my mind. I'm sorry. I just assumed. . ."

It was now his turn to cut her off. "You assumed right. I want to be alone with you more than you know. I just don't want you to do something you'll regret later."

She took a moment to answer. "I'm sure I'll regret this night no matter what we do. If we go home, I'll regret not having been with you. If we go to your room, I'll feel strange tomorrow. I've never done casual sex."

Slade lifted his glass. "Casual sex isn't all it's cut out to be. But I can tell you if we go up, it won't be casual. I like you, Nicole. Read into that anything you want, but I feel as though I've known you forever and I want to continue to get to know you."

Nicole felt tears burn her eyes. She looked down at the table feeling foolish, yet feeling strangely free and comfortable with this man. "I'd like to see your room and we can go from there."

Slade smiled as if he understood how she felt. "That sounds like a plan. We can see where this leads. No pushing."

"Thank you," Nicole said as she got up on her own. "Let's go before my brain tells me what I'm doing is wrong."

"It's not wrong. We simply want to know it's the right time."

The elevator ride down just two floors took an eternity. She held her purse close to her chest not daring to look at Slade. Maybe she was making a mistake. Maybe she should stop the elevator and make him take her home.

When the door slid open, she stepped out and Slade followed, but instead of heading down the hallway, he turned and pulled her into his arms.

She let out a big breath and melted against his chest.

He held her tightly against his body. "You okay?" he whispered.

"I am now." She didn't want to move, but when she realized her fingers had a death-grip around his sleeves, she eased slightly away from him.

He lifted her chin with his finger and kissed her gently. "I am too. I love having you in my arms."

"And I love being there, but let's get out of this hall before I panic and head back into the elevator."

He laughed. "I love your honesty." With his arm still around her shoulders, he led her all the way down the hallway to the last room, used the keycard and opened the door.

Nicole stood for a second, looked up at him, smiled, then walked past him. Stopping she took in the suite. Browns and shades of white with hints of gold spread across the room in the window treatments and on the chairs and couches. Obviously the bed was tucked away in the adjoining room. "This is beautiful."

"It is, isn't it? Again I have to thank my secretary."

She walked to the window and he followed.

Nicole took in the view of the Mississippi Sound below her. "The view is gorgeous."

He pulled her to his side. It felt so natural to be here with him and to be next to him.

"I love the lights from the boats just off shore," he continued. "When I leave my brother's restaurant in the evening, I like to pour a glass of wine and take all this in. My place in New York has a beautiful view of the skyline, but nothing like this."

"Tony took me to the city the first time we went up to visit his parents. The skyline at night is breathtaking. We did the tourist bit. I loved it, but I have to say I'm not sure I could live with all that traffic."

He nodded. "There aren't a lot of people who relish the traffic. You learn to walk or to take a lot of taxis. I never drive."

Nicole put her head against his shoulder and he

squeezed her.

"Now that you've seen the room's décor and the view from here, if you want we can go back to the restaurant or the lounge and have a drink then go home. I want you to be comfortable."

"There you go again trying to change my mind." She stepped out of his arms and faced him. "Maybe I should be asking you if that's what you'd rather do. You don't seem too excited about having me up here."

He pulled her back into his arms. "Are you kidding? Having you in my room and in my arms is a dream come true for me. Right now I feel like the luckiest man in the world just knowing you considered coming in here with me, and I *will* be the luckiest man in the world if you want to stay."

He held her tight again, just as he'd done in the hallway, but this time she lifted her face. With only inches from his lips, she felt his warm breath on her skin. He placed both of his hands on her face. Lowering his head he kissed her gently on the lips then moved his mouth to one cheek and then the other.

She clung to him as if her life depended on it. Savored the feeling of warmth and need spreading through her body.

She turned her head and captured his mouth in hers. He didn't disappoint. His lips were warm, but hard, and he kissed her with an intensity that took her breath away. She opened her mouth and let him explore. She did the same.

But she wanted more, more of him. All of him.

Did he realize what a big step this was for her, and more importantly, could she actually go through with it?

She pushed that thought aside, refusing to overthink what she wanted to do.

Reluctantly she pulled away slightly. "Am I going to have to beg you to take me to the bed?"

He smiled. "That might be nice. I've never had a lady beg me to take her to bed."

"Slade. . ."

He stopped her. "I wouldn't be so cruel, no matter how neat that would be." He took her hand, but after only one step, turned around and kissed her again, this time hard and consuming.

With his lips on hers and his hands caressing her, Nicole's thoughts scattered, but not so much she didn't know what she wanted. Her body burned. Her legs wobbled.

She threw her head back and moaned. When he moved his mouth to her neck, she pulled him closer hoping her legs wouldn't give way. Her entire body tingled and craved more.

"Slade." She managed to say his name before he straightened up and claimed her mouth again. Before she was able to form another word, he scooped her up. She threw her arms around his neck, kissed him back but she wanted to see where he was taking her. She needed to feel and to experience the entire moment. She wanted to see the bedroom and to see the bed, but she couldn't get past his dark eyes. They were opened as hers were.

"You're beautiful." His voice was deep, almost gravelly. "You have no idea how much this means to me."

She tried to answer, to tell him just how much it would mean to her as well, but he stopped moving.

She knew they were at the side of the bed and she prayed the panic wouldn't ruin her experience.

It didn't. Even as her body buzzed with anticipation, she felt a calm she hadn't experienced in a long time.

She looked up into his eyes and swallowed. He was smiling as he leaned down and kissed her gently, then placed her on the bed. Reaching up, she caressed his face. "Please don't make me wait. Make love to me."

~

Slade had wanted to make her wait. He wanted to extend the experience as long as he could, but hearing her ask him to make love to her blew him away. He tried, really tried, to make the moment last, but Nicole was as ready as he was. It was too fast, but wonderful.

Now with his heart still pounding against his chest, and his breath still coming in short gulps, he managed to open his eyes. Nicole lay under him with her eyes open. A tiny smile creased her lips.

He didn't want to move, but he knew his weight was still on her. He eased off, lay on his side, then pulled Nicole to him. "Thank you."

She raised her head. "Thank you? You're thanking me for making love to you."

"I'm thanking you for keeping up with me. It wasn't my finest hour. Oh wait, maybe I ought to say my finest three minutes."

She laughed. "If you noticed, three minutes was about what it took me."

"It's been a while for me," he said. "I'm sorry this didn't last all night long. I wanted to take it slow and make it wonderful for you. Instead, you drove me crazy."

She pulled his face to her and kissed him hard. He

felt his body wanting her again, but Nicole smiled. "It was wonderful for me, Slade, more than you'll ever know."

He watched her struggle for words. He didn't rush her to finish.

"You do know it's been even longer for me. Tony's been gone for three years."

"I'm sorry. Certainly I remember, and don't think for a moment that I thought you'd done this a lot."

"A lot?" She chuckled. "Try never. It's been hard for me to even look at another man until you walked into my café that first day."

"Aaah, then you didn't just see that young obnoxious jock walk it. That's a relief." His smile nearly did her in.

"Maybe."

"Ah baby, I told you you'd make me the luckiest man in the world, but I can assure you, you've done more than that. I'm honored you chose me. I'm not sure why you did, but I'm glad you did."

"I'm glad I did too. I should be thanking you. I thought I'd be terrified, but I didn't have time to think about anything else but you and what you were doing to me."

"Yeah, I kind of remember the same thing." He lowered his face to hers. "Maybe this time we can take it a little slower."

Chapter Twelve

Nicole opened her eyes. It took a second before she realized she was in Slade's hotel room in his bed. Turning, she saw him sound asleep next to her. She inhaled deeply and waited for the regret to consume her.
It didn't.
In fact, she felt better at this moment than she had in a long, long time.
She watched Slade sleep. His dark eye lashes lay against his cheeks, his lips unmoving, his breaths coming soft and even. A chill ran down her body remembering how his eyes seemed to devour her during the night with an intensity she wished she could experience now.
Pulling her gaze away from him, she glanced at the clock. 1:45. As much as she'd love to wake him with kisses, she knew she had to get back home. Still she wondered what he would do if she woke him ready to make love again.

Nicole smiled, savoring the moment before she had to go back to reality.

She eased herself out of the bed and crept to the bathroom to wash up before she woke him. When she came out, she tiptoed around the bed to pick up her clothes. She smiled remembering how he had undressed her slowly, kissing each part of her exposed body, driving her crazy and making her want him more. She picked up his clothes and almost laughed at how he had taken his time to undress her but had torn his clothes off of his body and tossed them.

She carried an armful of both his and her clothing into the bathroom to try to straighten the clothes before waking Slade. She left open the opportunity for him to make love to her once more. Smiling, she hand pressed his shirt and laid it on a countertop, then straightened the slacks. As she did so, several items fell out of his pocket. She stooped down to pick up his wallet that lay open with several business cards sticking out. Not wanting to be nosey she pushed them back into his wallet, but then stopped. The three cards were all the same and surprisingly familiar. Were they his business cards?

She knew he'd never given her a card, but she also knew she'd seen that logo before. *None of your business. Don't be nosey.*

Convincing herself she wasn't being nosey, just curious as to why the distinct black logo on the light blue background looked so familiar, she pulled one of the cards out once more. She had seen this card before. But where?

She flipped on a brighter light to be able to read the wording: New York Merger and Acquisitions. Her breath caught in her throat.

The realization took her breath away. Dropping the card on the countertop, she wrung her hands. Was it possible? Did Slade actually own the company that had bought the restaurant from her and Tony? Was he now the owner of The Yellow Rooster?

No. She refused to believe this man who had made such tender love to her just hours ago could possibly be the man who bought her property and kept the secret from her. Why didn't he just come right out and tell her?

He had never told her he wasn't the owner of The Yellow Rooster, but over and over had given her that impression. She looked at the card closer. Maybe she was mistaken. Maybe that wasn't the name of the company that had taken over hers and Tony's lounge.

Staring at the card for a long time wasn't doing anything but twisting her insides. The name was the same. The card was the same. A person doesn't forget something as devastating as selling a late husband's dream. She remembered every single moment of the transaction—signing paper after paper—staring at the tiny sum she was being paid—wondering why the real owners were not there to meet her and to introduce themselves to the community.

Now it all made sense. Slade Larson didn't want to be known as the person taking advantage of a young widow.

Quickly, she pulled on her clothes, ran a comb through her hair, took one of the cards and his clothes, then walked into the bedroom. Slade still slept.

She didn't want to confront him. She didn't want to know the truth, but she had to hear what he had to say.

She dropped his clothes on the bed, then flipped on the lamp on his side of the bed. He rolled over, smiled and held out his arms for her to come to him.

"You're dressed." He opened his eyes wider. "I was hoping you'd want to crawl back in here with me for a little while." He threw the blanket off.

Nicole swallowed as she looked at his naked body. He was ready for her again, and as much as she'd love to feel him against her, she shook her head.

"We need to talk." She took a step away from the bed. Distance from him would make this easier to take.

Slade frowned, then sat up on the side of the bed. "Nicole, what's wrong? I thought you were okay with what we did. I thought. . ."

"I was okay with everything we did. I loved making love to you. I woke up a little while ago feeling better than I had in years, and I wanted you to make love to make again."

"So why aren't we? I don't understand. You look upset."

She held out the business card. "You need to explain this. I picked up your clothes and it fell out." She wanted to say more, but a lump formed in her throat.

Slade closed his eyes for a minute, took a big breath and got up. He stood up and pulled his pants on before he faced her.

"Is this your business? Do you own The Yellow Rooster?" She blurted out the questions.

He took a step toward her and put his hands on her arms. "Let's go in the other room. We do need to talk."

"No, we don't need to go into the other room. You need to tell me now. Do you own The Yellow Rooster?

Is it you who bought the restaurant from me?"

"Yes, I do own it, or at least I'm part-owner. Gary is my partner. I gave him part ownership so he could run the business and have free rein because I couldn't be down here."

"Couldn't be or didn't want to be? Does Mac know? Does he know his brother owns the competition that's taking business away from Slade's?"

Slade nodded. "Yes, he knows.

"So both of you have been lying to me or at least dancing around the truth."

He dropped his arms to his side and turned away from her. "It wasn't supposed to be such a big deal. I saw an opportunity when I was here the year your restaurant and lounge went up for sale. My company was new and this was one of my first acquisitions. Eventually I was going to sell my share to Gary, but he is doing such a great job, I couldn't make myself do that to him until I was sure he was on his feet. He's the worker, the backbone of the business, but right now he needs my financial backing."

He turned back around and faced her. "I didn't know you then. Had I met you, things would've been different."

"How different? Just because you now know me doesn't make a bit of difference. You took advantage of a bad situation. Had it not been me, it would've been someone else down on their luck. The end would've been the same. Someone lost a business and you made a profit." She shook her head. "I can't believe I didn't see through you."

She turned and walked into the other room. He followed.

"Don't leave, Nicole. Please let me make this right?"

"You can't make this right. The damage is done." She walked toward the door, then turned back again. "I really thought we might have something together. I loved being with you and having you in my life for these few weeks. . ."

"Then it doesn't need to end. I loved being in your life and in Em's life. I want this to work. I told you this wouldn't be a casual night if you stayed and I meant it. Making love to you meant the world to me."

"And it did to me as well, but you don't get it, do you? You can't have a relationship if there isn't honesty in it. A couple has to trust each other."

"Nicole, I never lied to you."

"You're right. You never said the words. You simply waltzed around the truth and let me believe what I wanted. That's not grounds for trusting another person."

"I'm a businessman. It's how the world survives."

She threw her shoulders back. "Maybe in your world. Not in mine."

"I didn't mean to hurt you. I wanted to tell you several times about the restaurant, but the timing never seemed right. I didn't want to ruin my chances with you."

"Well, the timing is right now for me to go." She picked up her purse. "Don't bother to follow me down. I'll call my own cab."

"Please. Don't leave like this."

But it was too late. She was already in the hall. At first she stopped outside his door wanting more than anything to run back in and throw herself in his arms, but that could never be. Finally she headed to the elevator feeling worse than she had in years. She heard his door open, but she refused to look back.

When she stepped into the elevator, she had to turn. That's when she looked out and saw him standing in the hallway. He was the same man who had made her feel alive and like a woman again, but he was the man who had made her life's situation harder than it should have been when his company bought the lounge for so little, but worse, he had not been honest with her.

He stood by his door wearing only his pants, reminding her how she'd placed her head next to his chest. She'd loved the feel of the hair on his chest against her skin. She loved him.

As the elevator door started to close, she stared at him, never breaking their gaze. When it shut, she knew it was shutting Slade Larson out of her life for good.

~

Slade watched the elevator door shut, but he couldn't make himself move. He stood alone in the quiet hallway not believing the situation happened the way it had. Just as he'd told her, he had every intention of telling her about The Yellow Rooster, but no time seemed right, or maybe he hadn't wanted to see the look on her face when he told her. Now, his plan to explain the acquisition of her place went down the drain. She didn't believe he was going to tell her, and he was afraid she'd never believe him again.

He stepped into his room, slammed the door behind him, stomped into the bath, but stopped abruptly when he faced his image in the mirror. Who was this man? Where had the honest, hard-working Slade Larson gone? Once his goal was to help businessmen get back on their feet when they were down on their luck. What happened to that man?

He stared into the mirror for a long time. What seemed like such an innocent business deal three years ago now was exploding in his face. He really thought he was helping the widow by buying her property, and it wasn't supposed to be a major competition for his brother's lounge.

Still, even then, in the back of his mind a tiny voice had nipped at his consciousness. He had made the purchase using a representative rather than appearing in person. His schedule was packed that week, and he couldn't get down to the closing, but there had been many other opportunities. He chose not to get involved. He knew his brainchild and Gary's hard work would make an impact on the tourist community in Marsh Isles.

Did he really know it would be a problem for his brother and the other small businesses? Is that why he did it on the sly?

He had to admit that he had. He closed his eyes and dropped his head.

I just screwed up my life with the woman I was falling in love with.

He opened his eyes and stared into the mirror. Was he really falling in love with Nicole? The realization that it was possible took his breath away. He had never let himself get into a serious relationship with a woman, but Nicole and Em had sneaked into his life and in his heart. It had been a long time since he'd felt so at peace with himself and with life. Marsh Isles was starting to feel like home to him again.

Maybe he was destined to be a loner.

Maybe that's what he deserved.

~

The taxi pulled up in front of Nicole's house. When she'd left the house earlier with Slade, she had turned on the porch light and a small light in the living room. Now she stared at a mostly dark house. She held her purse on her lap and sat still in the back of the taxi. How could she go inside all alone to face what had happened tonight? Earlier when she'd been with Slade she knew she would eventually come home alone, but she'd have wonderful memories to keep her company. Now what did she have?

"Ma'am? Is this the right address?"

"Oh yes. I'm sorry." She pulled out money from her purse and paid the taxi driver, giving him a nice tip.

She walked to the door, unlocked it, but couldn't make herself go inside to face the inevitable loneliness waiting her. Instead she flipped off the porch light, tossed her purse on a chair, then stepped back onto the porch and sat on the swing with only the dim light shining through the window.

Her neighbors slept at this time of the night. No movement. No noise. No traffic. She felt totally alone.

She wondered what Slade was doing. Was he still awake or had he immediately fallen back asleep? Did he understand why she'd stomped out of his room?

She pushed herself on the swing and let the slow back-and-forth movement calm her.

From inside the house she heard her phone ring. She ran inside and grabbed it thinking it was Miss Tillie needing her help, but when she looked at the name, it was Slade.

She stared at the phone and listened to the ringtone

without answering it. Finally it went to Voice Mail. She took the phone to the swing and held it to her chest until she heard the familiar beep signaling the message was complete.

Could she listen to it? Did she want to hear what Slade had to say?

Before she talked herself out of it, she hit the message indicator. "Nicole, this is Slade. Please call me. I need to talk with you. I should've never let you walk away tonight. Please call." There was a long pause. "I don't want our time together to end like this." Again, there was a pause, then he hung up.

For a long time she stared at the phone wanting more than anything to call him, to tell him she forgave him and to tell him she loved him, but she couldn't. Honesty was necessary in a relationship, and he obviously didn't believe that or didn't understand it. She thought she had started to know Slade, but now she realized he hadn't shown her the real Slade Larson.

Leaning back against the swing, she tried to reconcile all that had happened since she'd driven off from here with Slade just hours ago. How could such a wonderful, absolutely ecstatic night turn into such a nightmare?

She had made love to Slade, giving herself entirely to him, and now—now she wasn't sure what to do. She knew she could never trust him again even though in her heart she knew she had fallen in love with him.

How could that be? After losing Tony she didn't think she could ever love again, but she'd opened her heart to Slade and allowed him into hers and Em's life—and look where it got her.

A horrible thought struck her. How was she going

to explain to Em that Slade was no longer in their lives? How many times had her daughter mentioned wanting him or Mr. Mac as her new daddy?

    She dropped her head into her hands and rested it on her knees. *What have I done to my daughter?*

Chapter Thirteen

The next afternoon between the lunch and dinner hours, Nicole left Clark in charge of her café and headed to Slade's Restaurant. She needed to talk with Mac. She'd called earlier and spoke to James, the barback, who told her he thought Slade had gone to New York, so she knew she wouldn't run into him. She wasn't ready to face him or talk with him. She needed time to deal with all that she'd found out.

James was stocking the bar when she went inside. "Hey, James. Is Mac here yet?"

James looked up from the counter. "He's in his office, but I have to warn you, he's not in a very good mood. It's none of my business, but I think he and his brother had it out this morning."

"I'm sorry to hear that, but I'll take my chances with him."

She heard him chuckle and throw in a "good luck" as she passed the bar.

When she knocked on the office door, Mac's gruff

voice started her. "James, I told you I didn't want to talk to anyone."

"Mac, it's me. Nicole. I'd like to talk with you."

Mac didn't answer. She let out a big breath. James was probably right. Mac was upset. She decided to try later, but before she left, the door jerked open. She looked up but Mac had already turned and headed back to his desk.

At least he had opened the door. "Do you have time to talk?"

Mac didn't answer so Nicole stepped inside the office. Mac threw himself in his desk chair, huffed out a big breath and stared at her. "I guess."

"Good." Nicole took a seat in front of his desk. "I'd like to talk about Slade."

"Not a good subject today."

"I'm assuming he told you what took place last night?"

About The Yellow Rooster and not about our love making.

"He told me. Nicole, I'm so sorry my little brother deceived you about the restaurant he bought from you and Tony."

"So you knew it was his company that bought it."

Mac looked up. "Yes, but it never occurred to me that you didn't. The less I thought about that place the better. I knew it was going to be a huge success."

"I figured it out last night when I saw his business card." She slumped back in the chair. "I was devastated. Not just because it was his company that bought the lounge—somebody would've eventually bought it—but because he led me to believe he wasn't associated with it."

"Yeah, that brother of mine has no heart, no soul, and no sense of loyalty."

Nicole swallowed. "At first I thought the same thing. I didn't trust him, and until last night he had convinced me he was a pretty decent man. Maybe it was all a show, but I really thought he cared about Em and me."

Nicole quit talking. Saying the words hurt. She thought she had gotten the emotions out of her this morning when she'd told Miss Tillie. In her gentle understanding way, Miss Tillie had held her and let her cry on her shoulder, but obviously she wasn't completely as ready as she thought to talk about it with Mac.

"Nicole, I'm so sorry. I wouldn't have asked him to come down here to help me with this restaurant if I'd known it was going to give you problems. I guess he laughed at the state this business is in. His big city ways and all of his money don't fit in down here."

"I don't think he'd make fun of what you're doing here, Mac. Slade loves you and has a great admiration for you, and believe it or not, he wanted to save the restaurant. I'm sure he bought The Yellow Rooster not thinking it would cause anyone any problems."

"That's what he said, but he was wrong, wasn't he?" Mac got up, shoved his chair against the wall and walked around the desk. "I'm sorry. You don't need to hear all this. You have your own situation to deal with."

She nodded, fighting to hold back the tears.

"Slade said some things this morning," he said, "that makes me think he was falling for you. I'd already figured that out, but watching him admit what he had done to you was an eye opener. I wanted to strangle him for buying that lounge when it took place, but listening to him this morning made me almost feel sorry for him. He was miserable when he headed back to New York."

She let Mac's words sink in. Slade did have feelings for her. She closed her eyes and tried to breathe.

"Are you okay, Nicole?"

She nodded. "I think I am, but maybe I'm not. You know since Tony died I haven't even looked at another man, but Slade was different. I was falling for him as well, and Em absolutely loved him. She's old enough to realize he won't be around and I'm not sure what I'll tell her."

"I'm so sorry it's someone in my family making your life miserable. You deserve so much more than that."

Nicole stood up. "I'm a big girl. I'll get over it. I've got too much on my mind most of the time with Em's health to think about being with anyone. I guess I let myself get a little selfish when I was with Slade. It felt good to have someone at my side again."

"No. Not selfish. Just human. If he added a little sunshine to your life, then I'm happy, but I can't understand him ripping it away like he did. Do you think you can ever forgive him?"

She shrugged. "Maybe. Like I said I have a lot of other stuff on my mind right now. My social life is the least of my worries."

"How is Emily? I know she ended up in the hospital last month. Is she doing better?"

"She has a lot of good days, but it only takes one bad episode for me to start wondering what I'm going to do in the future. It's getting harder and harder for her to get over these episodes."

"Is her doctor talking about when she'll need some of those new treatments that are available?"

"We're always talking about that. Dr. Murry, her blood specialist and I are all checking into different programs that could take her. I'm struggling to pay for health insurance, and it's not very good, but I'm not going to let that stand in the way. I'll find a way." She reached out and took his hand. "Thanks for being here for me when I need you. I'm sorry I'm the one who made Slade return to New York."

"No, Nicole, it wasn't only you. He left because he couldn't face me or you. I'm not even sure why we were arguing this morning. I think he needed to unload on someone and who better than his brother. He'll come around. He's my brother. We always get over our squabbles. I think he realized I was about to physically toss him out, but he decided to leave on his own. Of course, I'm sure he knew I'd probably hurt myself trying to kick him out of here. He's in a little better shape than I'm in."

For the first time since Nicole had come into his office, Mac laughed.

She laughed with him. "Oh, I don't know about that. You're in pretty good shape for all you do around here and the hours you keep. I just hate to see brothers have problems. Family should be everything."

"This isn't our first falling out and it won't be our last." He stepped near her and pulled into his arms. "If there's anything I can do for you, let me know."

"Thank you. It's nice to know I can depend on you. You're like the brother I never had."

"I feel honored." He stepped away.

"I'd better get to work here. I left Clark in charge and he's pretty new."

She left Mac's office feeling a little better than when she'd come in. Just hearing Mac say the words that Slade was falling for her warmed her heart, but at the same time made her angry. Why hadn't he told her about The Yellow Rooster earlier? Maybe there would have been a chance for them. Things would've been strained, but there wouldn't have been any anger. Now things were different.

She thought about the possibility of what might have been. They could've been good together.

Now it was gone.

~

Slade flagged a taxi, then gave the driver his office address. He leaned back against the rough backseat and wondered what possessed him to come back to New York City. He didn't want to be here and didn't need to be here. He should be in Marsh Isles sitting on a certain someone's front porch reveling in the time they'd spent together the night before, not sitting in some taxi heading to his office.

He looked out the window at the dreary weather and the workers bundled up hurrying to work. He wished the weather would've been better so he could've walked this morning, but the temperature had dropped into the forties with a light rain, much too nasty for him to walk.

Maybe he had gotten used to the coastal warmth. He closed his eyes. He'd gotten used to a lot of other things and now they were gone.

Walking may have helped to clear his mind after the sleepless hours he'd spent last night. It was almost midnight by the time he landed, made his way by rote through the airport, then got a taxi to his condo. He opened the door, dropped his suitcase and stared at the empty room. The spacious floorplan and breathtaking views of the city's skyline didn't do anything but emphasize the loneliness he'd fought with during the flight back to New York.

Sitting in the Atlanta airport during his layover, he almost switched flights and gone back. There was so much he needed to say to Nicole. He'd even driven by her house and knocked on her door before heading to the airport, but she wasn't home. He swung by the café, but an early lunch crowd was already inside. No way could he talk to her in front of all those people. Now she wasn't even answering his phone calls.

Not that he blamed her.

All night he had gone over different scenarios, but they all ended the same. Nicole had left him standing in the hotel hallway alone. Her reaction threw him for a loop. He'd expected her to be upset over his not telling her about his ownership of The Yellow Rooster, but he had no idea she would be so hurt and angry.

She'd told him he couldn't be trusted. That hurt. He was the most trustworthy and honest person amongst his fellow businessmen. His reputation was spotless. Never in his entire life had he ever done anything dishonest, but now he had lost Nicole for what she considered dishonesty—and maybe he had been.

He wanted to punch something because he knew it would take a miracle for her to place her trust in him again.

Watching her walk away last night after making love to her was almost surreal. In a matter of minutes they went from being lovers to her turning against him and leaving him. Now he was doing the only thing that got him through his recent adult life. He was going to work.

"Here we are, sir." The cab driver told him the amount, accepted the money, then went around to open the door for Slade, though he had already exited the taxi.

"Thanks," Slade said as he walked to the door of the office building. The warm interior felt great. *Yep, I'm getting soft.*

"Good morning, Mr. Larson. It's nice to see you back." The receptionist for the building greeted him as if nothing important had happened or had changed in his life.

"Good morning to you. It's nice to be back." No need to give all the gory details about why he cut his trip short.

He caught the elevator and headed up to his office hating the fact that Kelli was going to have a million questions. He had no intentions of answering any of them.

Kelli sat behind her desk with a stack of folders in front of her, working as diligently as if he had been keeping an eye on her from the other room. *How did I ever get so lucky with this lady? Too bad I can't be as lucky with a lady I love.*

"Mr. Larson, you're back early." She sat up straight and smiled. "I had no idea you'd be here today, or did I?" She got serious. "Surely I didn't forget."

Slade smiled. "No, you didn't forget. I decided to come back last night. I even changed my ticket and arranged everything myself."

She laughed. "I don't believe it."

"Believe. It's amazing what we men can do on our own." He headed to his office, but turned around. "But don't get any ideas. You do my schedules and flights perfectly. I like it that way much better."

Her gaze seemed to burn into his back as he walked into his office and he could almost hear the thousand questions she wanted to ask about why he was here so early. He closed the door behind him and wished he was brave enough to confide in her. They'd been working together for years. He knew he owed her an explanation, but what would he say? How do you tell someone who was more than a secretary that he'd screwed up his life? If he actually said the words out loud they would make his situation true.

For an hour he went over the work that Kelli had kept him up on while he was on the coast. There wasn't much he had to do but he stayed at his desk even after he'd finished and now stared out the window at the typical scene of New Yorkers scurrying through the streets.

Someone knocked at the door. He knew it was Kelli and for a moment he thought about not answering it. She knocked again.

"Come in," he said and even he recognized the monotone of his voice.

"Slade, is everything okay?"

Kelli hardly ever used his first name, but when she did it meant she looked at him as more than a boss. They were close friends even though they never socialized alone outside of work. She was happily married and several times he had joined her and her husband for dinner. He always loved seeing them together and sharing time with them. Theirs was one of the few marriages he knew of that actually worked.

"I guess you won't believe me if I tell you everything is fine."

"Nope, I won't." She sat down. "You know I don't like to pry into your personal affairs, but sometimes friends need to do just that."

Slade smiled. "Yes, I guess friends do just that." He wasn't sure where to start. Rubbing his hand across the back of his neck, he looked at her, then stood up and walked to the window. "You know the acquisition we made a few years ago in Marsh Isles?"

"Of course I do. Did something happen to it?"

"Nope, it's getting stronger every season and Gary is doing a wonderful job. It was one of the best deals I've ever made."

"So?"

Slade chuckled. Kelli understood him so well. "So, the acquisition that is turning into a goldmine for Gary and me has turned into a personal problem."

Kelli didn't say anything. She leaned back in her chair and waited.

"I guess you're not going to be satisfied until I tell you all the unpleasant details of what happened."

"You're right. I'm not."

Slade started his story, but couldn't look at the woman who had been with him from the beginning of his company. She'd seen him at his best and at his worst. She watched him climb the ladder of success with hard work and personal sacrifices and stuck by him through it all. Now she listened as he told her the entire story, all of it, even the part about Nicole and Em. He left out the part of about them making love, but from her look he felt sure she knew.

"She was the widow you bought the lounge from?"

"Yep. Who knew my first acquisition would come back to bite me?"

"That's a coincidence if I'd ever heard one." She sat up straight. "So what now? Did you try to call her? Should you go back down there?"

"To answer your questions: Yes and probably not. I tried to call a bunch of times but she won't answer. If I thought she wouldn't call the police to get me off her porch, I'd fly back down there today."

Kelli got up and walked up next to him and placed a hand on his arm. "I've never seen you like this, Slade. I have a feeling my friend fell in love."

He didn't answer.

"Okay. No answer is an answer as well. What can I do?"

"What can anyone do at this point? I thought I'd give her some time to cool off and maybe remember that she was falling for me as well, or at least that's what she told me. If I knew how to have her forgive me, I'd do it this instance. Same goes for Mac. When I told him about how Nicole reacted to her finding out, I thought he was going to slug me. He thought I had already told her."

Slade finally stepped away from the window and faced Kelli. "I wish he would've hit me. Buying that place was a business deal, a really good deal for my new company at the time, and it was never supposed to hurt anyone. I guess I wasn't thinking too straight."

"I'm so sorry. Time might help with Nicole and with Mac. You know he's your brother. He'll come around as well."

"I hope so because my time down there made me realize how much I love my brother and how much I miss being with him. I even thought about getting more involved with the business, but now I guess none of that means anything."

"It means something. It means a lot. He'll come around because he loves you. He's your brother and will always be. Don't give up on him. You didn't do anything to him. He's mad because of how all this has affected Nicole." She took a big breath. "I'm going back to work. If you need to take some time off, I'll call you if I need you here."

Slade laughed. "You sound like the boss. No, I'm okay. I need to be right here for the moment, but thanks."

She got to the door and turned. "Don't give up on Nicole either. You're a good man and I'm sure she knows that even though right now she's a little peeved with you. Give her time."

When Kelli left him alone again, he picked up his phone, hit Nicole's number and left her another message. Before he hung up, he added a last thought. "Nicole, if you or Em needs me, please don't let all this stand in the way. I'm here for you." He wanted to add "I love you," but he wasn't sure that would help the situation.

Instead, he simply asked her to call him back, knowing she wouldn't.

Chapter Fourteen

"Mama, you made spaghetti. I love spaghetti." Nicole placed a bowl in front of Em. "I did because you've been so good this week, I thought you deserved it."

"I do, huh?" She giggled.

Nicole poured a glass of milk for Em and a glass of tea for herself before sitting down. Her helping of spaghetti was almost non-existent. She knew she needed to eat, especially being at the table with Em, but the thought of swallowing food nearly choked her. Since Slade's revelation, it was hard for her to function.

She hated what Slade did, but realized she still loved the man and didn't know what to do about that. And Em. How would she tell her daughter?

She'd left her café early again to be with Em. Now that she was home, she needed to explain to Em that Slade wouldn't be in their lives anymore, and do it in such a way that she wouldn't be upset. One day she might see Slade again and she didn't want her daughter to hold any bad thoughts against him.

She'd thought long and hard if she should say anything to Em and how she could make herself say the words. Now she watched her daughter suck in long strands of pasta and hoped she wouldn't back out.

"Em, Mr. Slade said to tell you good-bye. He had to go back to New York."

Slade had not mentioned Em when Nicole had left the apartment. *A little fib wouldn't hurt.* Of course, he did mention her in his last telephone message.

Em put her fork down. "He left? He didn't tell me good-bye and pick me up and spin me around like he always does."

"I know. He had to get back to work."

"When's he coming back to town? He said we'd play and he always does what he says."

This was harder than Nicole thought it would be. She hated lying to her daughter, but no way would she tell her the truth about what had happened.

"He wasn't sure. In fact, he wasn't sure he'd be back here any time soon. He came to Marsh Isles to help his brother and that job is done. He's a very busy man in New York where he lives and he had to leave."

Em frowned then picked up her glass of milk and took a big swallow. "He was busy before but he had time to play with us."

Em's statement amazed Nicole. How could someone so young understand so much?

"He did, didn't he? We'll have to wait and see. Grown men have to go to work and make money. They have lots of responsibilities. Sometimes it's hard for them to find time to play."

"Mr. Slade did though." She took a big bite of

spaghetti. "He'll be back. He loves me."
Tears burned the back of Nicole's eyes. *I thought he loved me too.*

~

The next morning after getting everything organized at her café, Nicole walked across the street to The Yellow Rooster. She wasn't sure why she had to do this, but she did. She stood inside the dim light of the lounge and took a minute to catch her breath before she came face to face with Gary.

Now that she knew Slade owned this lounge, she looked at her surroundings in a different light. Before, it had been a reminder of the renovations she and Tony wanted to do, but couldn't afford. Now she knew the lounge was the brainchild of Slade. Even though she knew that Gary had done most of the work, she had a feeling Slade was behind a lot of it.

She wondered if Slade had picked out the new furniture or had an input into the best bandstand she'd ever seen. Or the new front door. Or the unique sign in the front.

Oooh, what am I doing here?

"Hey, Nicole." Gary's deep voice came from behind her before she was able to make her escape.

She turned around. Gary carried two boxes out of the kitchen and headed toward the bar.

"Hey, Gary. I wanted to walk over before you opened, but I wasn't sure if Slade left orders to throw me out if I did."

Gary chuckled. "Why would he do that? You're the one who had reason not to ever show up here again. He shouldn't be upset with you."

"So he told you we had a little argument? How was

he when you saw him?"

He put his boxes behind the bar then walked up alongside of her and put his arm around her, gave her a squeeze then took a step back. "Girl, I can tell you he was upset, but not with you. Slade Larson is a businessman who never shows his emotions. He can deal with anyone and slap on the best poker face around. Yesterday he wasn't anyone I recognized. I swear the man looked like a broken piece of, uh, a broken man."

Nicole smiled at the way he caught himself from saying anything that might sound offensive.

"I'm sorry to hear that. I like Slade. I don't like to make anyone feel bad. I guess I might have overreacted to the news of his buying this place from me, especially the way I found out." She looked into his eyes. "Did you know who I was when we first met? Did he tell you that this had been my husband's lounge? Slade was keeping it all a big secret from me, but I'm assuming you knew."

"Are you going to take your wrath out on me if I tell you I figured it out when I started redoing this place? Someone mentioned your name and your connection, but Slade didn't know you opened the café."

Nicole plopped down in a chair. "I feel like the only one in Marsh Isles who didn't know he owned the acquisition company."

"No, businessmen just accept buyouts. No one really cares who owns the big companies that buy failing businesses. Stuff like that happens all the time. It became old business the day the papers were signed. As far as anyone was concerned, I was the owner and manager."

Gary sat down. "Nicole, I can't defend the fact that he didn't tell you right away, but you have to know that Slade is a good man."

"I know he is. He showed that to me in his dealings with my daughter. I'm glad you're a part-owner."

"Yeah, me too. Slade gave me a partnership so I could run it and do what I want. I throw ideas out to him and he lets me know exactly how he feels about it. Sometimes we agree on my ideas. Sometimes we don't. Our partnership seems to work. I didn't have the money to invest and still don't. He doesn't have the time. "

"I can look around and see what your collaboration has accomplished. When Tony and I had this place, it didn't look anything like this. I guess you remember what a dump it was when Slade bought it."

"Oh, go easy on yourself. It wasn't that bad. It just needed a little work."

"A little? Gary, Tony had such wonderful ideas, but we never had the money to do any of it." She looked down at the floor. "When I look around today and see what you and Slade did here, it hurts to know that Tony never was able to fulfill his dream."

Gary reached out and took her hand. "It was your dream as well."

"Maybe or maybe I was just going along with my husband. Whatever the reason, it was a dream that didn't need to be fulfilled right then. It should've been put on a shelf until we had the money to invest. I should've been stronger and convinced him to wait." She straightened her shoulders and took a deep breath. "But that's not anyone's problem but mine." Nicole stood up. "I have to get back. If you hear from Slade, would you let me know how he's doing?"

"You know I will" He stood up and gave her a brotherly hug. "You and Slade will work this out."

"I don't know, Gary. I'm confused and really upset with him."

"It's none of my business, but I know Slade and I know enough about you to say you're both good people and you'll get through this."

Nicole went back to her café to open for the lunch hours. Throughout the day, her thoughts never left Slade. By the time the last lunch customer left, she pulled her phone from her purse, took a small cola from the bar, then walked out into the sunshine. She let herself relax a moment before she looked at the phone, assuming she'd have several calls from Slade.

There were none.

Disappointment filled her entire being. Had he given up on her? Should she have answered his earlier phone calls?

Of course she should have. She'd been a coward.

Would she answer his next call or should she finally call him? If she were honest with herself, she knew she should. She made the decision to call Slade, but not now. This wasn't the time or the place to call.

Now that she had decided to talk with him, her afternoon hours dragged by. By the time she walked out of the café and locked the back door, she almost ran to her Jeep. As soon as she got in, she pulled out her phone. Panic struck. What would she say? Should she blurt out that she loved him? That she forgave him? That she wanted to see him?

None of those were viable. She did love him. She did want to see him, but she wasn't sure she forgave him—at least for now. She needed time and she didn't want to be with someone who could not be trusted.

But she needed to hear his voice. She hit his contact before she changed his mind, listened to the phone ring, then realized he wasn't going to answer.

She hung up without leaving a message, then shoved the phone in her purse. Her heart actually hurt. She bit her lip not wanting to play through the scenarios of why he had not answered. Maybe he was in a meeting or maybe he simply stared at the phone as she had done when he'd called.

She pulled out onto the street and drove a couple of blocks before her phone buzzed. Seeing Slade's name, she pulled off the road not trusting herself to talk with him while she was driving. She answered it.

"Nicole, I'm so sorry I missed your call. I had my ringer off because I was with a client."

She didn't know what to say.

"You did call me, didn't you?"

Nicole took a big breath. "Yes. I did. I should've answered one of your earlier calls, but I didn't know what to say or if I was ready to hear what you had to say."

"And now you are?" he asked.

"I don't know. I just know it was rude to ignore you. Mac said you went back to New York."

"I did. Don't ask me why. It's not what I wanted to do, but I had a feeling you and Mac didn't want me around. I did go to your house before I left, but you weren't there. I really wanted to see you, Nicole. When I got to Atlanta I almost caught a plane back to the coast, but, well, here I am in New York."

"I still don't know how I feel about what you did.

No, that's not true. I do know how I feel. I'm hurt you kept that information from me. I know you didn't know me at first except from high school, but after we got to know each other again, you should've been able to talk with me."

"I know that now. Nicole, I swear, I tried to tell you several times, but it never felt like the right moment to do it. I was enjoying being with you and Em too much to ruin our time together. In my heart I knew you'd be angry."

"Hurt more than angry." She tried to get her thoughts together." I have to tell you I loved Tony, but after he died, I realized he'd kept things from me. It's made my life miserable and possibly put Em's at risk. I swore I'd never be with another man I couldn't trust."

"And I just reinforced that feeling," he said in a soft voice.

"Yes." The simple word seemed to shatter her world.

A long silence ensued before Slade's voice came through the phone.

"Do you think we can get through this? Will you give me a chance?"

"I don't know. I want to, but my head tells me to leave things as they are."

"I understand that, but what does your heart tell you?"

Nicole swallowed. Did she dare tell him how she really felt? Did she know how she felt?

"Today I'm not so sure. Had you asked me the other night my answer wouldn't been a definite . . . answer." She couldn't get the words of love out.

She heard him take a deep breath. "Okay. I deserve

that, but I don't want us to simply walk away from what I think we had."

"I have to think about Em. It's not only what I want. She already attached herself to you, and that's one reason I called. She wanted to know when you were coming to play with her. She said you loved her."

"Oh, Nicole, I do. When I get back to the coast, will you allow me to see her?"

"That's the thing. I don't want to give her a reason to be hurt if we can't get over this. I thought I'd let you know how she feels. Maybe I shouldn't have told you. I didn't know what to tell her."

"You tell her I will come to play with her as soon as I can, and of course, that will depend on you. I'd drop what I'm doing right now and catch a plane if you invited me back."

Nicole closed her eyes and dropped her head against the seat. Cars crept by her Jeep on her narrow neighborhood road but her world spun out of control.

"Are you still there?"

"Yes, I'm here," she whispered, "but I have to go. I'm on my way home."

"I'm so glad you called. I needed to hear your voice."

"Would you do me a favor and not call me for a while? I don't want that to sound mean. I simply need time alone to think through all this. I promise I'll call you when I can."

"That's not what I want to do."

"But it's what we need to do. Please, Slade. Give me a little time."

"If that's the only way, then, yes, I'll give you all the time you need. I'll let you get home. Kiss that girl of yours for me."

Nicole pressed the disconnect button but couldn't make her foot press the accelerator to head back home. She had done the right thing by calling Slade, but was it right to ask him not to call her? Not sure where that request had come from, she now had to live with it.

She knew she'd regret it. It was good to hear his voice.

How had she gotten her life in such a mess?

Chapter Fifteen

Nicole finally made her way home feeling as confused as she'd ever been. Miss Tillie met her on the front porch as usual.

"Where's Em?" Nicole asked as she climbed the steps.

"She's in her bed. I've been checking on her, but she's a little tired today."

"Oh no. Maybe I need to take her to the doctor." She looked at her watch. "Oh phooey, the office is closed."

Miss Tillie placed a hand on her arm. "I thought about calling, but I'm never sure when the time's right to involve the doctor."

"I know exactly what you mean. I either think I'm a bad mother for not paying attention to her signs or I think I'm a helicopter mom when I rush to conclusions thinking she's about to have a spell."

"I guess we're pretty normal. I think all mothers

face the same dilemma in trying to decide when a professional needs to be seen."

"Still that doesn't make me feel better when I overlook the signs and Em has a spell. I'll go check on her and see what she looks like. I'll call you and let you know how she is."

"No, I'll wait here. I'd like to hear what you think."

"Miss Tillie, don't feel you have to do that. I don't want to impose. You've been here all afternoon already."

"Would you go check on your daughter?" Miss Tillie pushed her rocker and looked straight ahead ignoring Nicole. "If I want to wait here, I certainly will."

Nicole laughed. "Thanks. I need you more than you know."

Nicole rushed into the house, threw her purse down and headed for Em's bedroom.

"Hi, Mama. You're home." Em sat up in her bed and picked up one of her dolls and hugged her tight."

Nicole tried not to be too obvious as she looked for all the signs of an episode starting to happen. Except for being a little pale, Em looked okay.

"Yep, I certainly am home and will be home all night. Are you hungry?"

"No. Miss Tillie let me have ice cream."

"Good for Miss Tillie. How about some spaghetti from yesterday? I'll be glad to warm it up."

"No, Miss Lucy and I aren't hungry. We had a tea party with our ice cream." She hugged her doll and slid back under the blanket.

"Em, are you feeling okay?"

She nodded.

"You know how sometimes you feel really tired and woozy and we go see Dr. Murry?"

Again Em simply nodded.

"If you feel that way, will you call me? I'm going to talk with Miss Tillie for a few minutes but I'll have the monitor on."

"Yes, ma'am, I will, but I don't want to go to the doctor."

"I know you don't." Nicole leaned over and kissed Em on the forehead, feeling to see if she had a fever while doing so. "Would it be okay if I sleep in your bed tonight?"

"Yes. We can have a slumber party."

Nicole barely heard her voice. She stood up and started to leave then turned back. "I talked to Mr. Slade today."

Em popped up her head. "You did! Did he say anything about me? Did he say he was coming to play with me?"

Nicole sat back on the side of the bed. "He said he'd try to get back here but he wasn't sure when that would be. He did say to tell you he loved you and to give you a big kiss for him."

Em opened her arms and Nicole leaned into her. After giving her a big kiss, she pulled slightly away.

"See, I told you he loved me."

Nicole pulled Em's blanket up to her chin and kissed her again. When Em closed her eyes, Nicole stood for a few minutes thinking about her words. Did Slade really love Em or was he simply using his relationship with her to get closer to Nicole? It was obvious how Em felt about him and that bothered her. What if she couldn't forgive Slade and had to walk away? Even if she forgave him would she ever trust him enough to have a relationship with him? Em had been through so much in her short life. Nicole hated to put her happiness at risk. Finally, she turned to go back on the porch.

"Well? What do you think?" Miss Tillie sat up straight in her rocker. "Was I being an overprotective old lady?"

"Absolutely not. She looks tired and a little pale. She's not running fever. I'm not going to call the doctor right now, but I think I'll sleep in the bed with her tonight."

"I can stay here if it makes you feel better."

"No, you go home and get a good night's sleep, but I swear I'll call you if she needs to go to the hospital."

Miss Tillie got up and hugged Nicole. "You're a good mother, Nicole. That little girl is lucky to have you."

Nicole hugged her back then plopped down in one of her rockers. "Most of the time I feel like I have no idea what I'm doing. I've even thought about moving to upper New York state so Tony's parents could help me. They have more resources than my mother."

"Would you be happy there?"

Nicole shook her head. "That's why I haven't done it before, but I keep thinking that one day I have to do more than this for Em. Her disease is not going to cure itself. And I'm not sure you and I can deal with it alone."

"When the time comes, you'll know what to do. Things have a way of heading you in the right direction."

"Let's hope so because I'm not sure what that

direction would be right now."

Nicole sat on the porch alone for a few minutes after Miss Tillie left letting her mind take in all that had happened over the last few days. As much as she hated not having Slade at her side, she knew Em's health took precedent in her life. If she was destined to be alone with her daughter, then so be it. She'd manage.

She closed her eyes. Having Slade next to her would be so reassuring. She wished she could turn back the clock to the happier time before she'd read his business card.

But that could never be. The fact remained she'd fallen for someone who didn't feel she deserved to know the truth and that hurt.

She'd deal with her feelings for Slade later. Right now her daughter needed her.

~

At 2:40 a.m. Nicole sat in the ER next to Em's bed waiting for her blood transfusion to be brought into the room. Em was in a deep sleep, deep enough to scare Nicole.

Miss Tillie walked into the room with two cups of coffee. Nicole took hers and sipped but didn't taste it.

Pulling a chair close to Nicole at Em's bedside, Miss Tillie took Em's hand and held it. "She'll be back to her old self as soon as they get that blood in her."

Nicole smiled. "I hope so, but I'm so scared this is the episode that Dr. Murry will tell me I have to take her someplace else." Nicole put her coffee down and crossed her arms across her chest. "I'm so scared and confused."

"I wish I had the magical words to make things better." Miss Tillie sat up straight and wrung her hands.

"You know my offer still stands. Whatever it takes to get her where she needs to be, I'll pay."

"I might have to take you up on that—as a loan of course. Dr. Murry checked into programs that might be right for her and right now there aren't any openings unless it's an emergency. I hate to leave the coast, but I'm afraid it's time."

Juggling her coffee cup, Miss Tillie put her arm around Nicole's shoulders and hugged her.

Nicole leaned into her arm. "I don't want to leave you, Miss Tillie. You're more of a grandmother than her real ones. Em doesn't even remember them."

"One day she'll get to know them. Who knows? Something good might come of all this, and since you can't sell this house, it will always be here for you to come back."

"You're right as usual. We'll hope for the best and deal with whatever comes our way, and Barry Keats is one of the things that will probably come our way much too soon. I'm surprised I haven't had any calls from him lately. I just can't believe he isn't making his usual phone calls."

Miss Tillie didn't say anything. Nicole looked at her. The lady's gaze went everywhere but at Nicole. Something wasn't right.

"Miss Tillie, do you know something I don't know?"

"I know a lot of things you don't know."

Nicole laughed. "Of course you do, but I was talking specifically about Barry Keats." She waited. "Is there something you're not telling me about this man?"

"Not really."

"Okay, that's not an answer. What do you mean?"

She wrinkled her nose. "I know my nephew at the police department was checking up on him after he passed our houses. We gave him the license plate number to see if he was someone we needed to be concerned about."

"We? Who's we?"

"Slade was as concerned about the man as I was. He's the one who got my nephew's name and had him checked out."

"I'm not sure how I feel about him getting into my personal life, but I have to ask, what did he find out?"

"As far as William could tell Mr. Keats doesn't have a record so he said you and I should keep an eye on him, but he really hasn't done anything to bring him in."

"It's good to know the man isn't some kind of horrible criminal."

"Yes, that's a good thing," Miss Tillie said.

Nicole was convinced the lady knew a lot more about Mr. Keats, but Em squirmed in the bed and both of them gave their attention to her. Within the hour Em's IV came in. Miss Tillie sat with her a little longer, then caught a taxi home.

By early morning Nicole sat next to Em's bed watching the IV that once more was giving her daughter lifesaving blood. They'd been in the hospital for seven hours already and Em had been given a private room. Dr. Murry came in at six and confirmed that it was time for Em to have more than transfusions. He gave her a list of possibilities, none of which were anywhere near the coast. Even though some of the hospitals had free services for children like Em, she knew she'd need money to get her there.

She looked at the list but didn't see anything but blurred letters. Her bank account showed a little savings, but that was to pay Barry Keats. Now she'd have to ask him once again for an extension. Surely the man had a heart and wouldn't deny a little girl the medical treatments that might save her life. If the man didn't have a heart, she'd have to ask Tony's family or Miss Tillie for a loan.

~

After leaving the hospital, Miss Tillie went home and tried to get some sleep, but she had too much on her mind to relax. She tossed and turned. Sleep did not come, but she did make some decisions. She couldn't wait around and do nothing.

After a light breakfast, she called a taxi and now sitting in the back seat, she wrung her hands as the driver took her to Slade's Restaurant. Nicole would not approve of what she was about to do, but she'd deal with her anger later.

She paid the taxi and marched into the restaurant. James directed her to Mac's office. With a quick knock, she walked in.

Mac looked up from his desk. "Miss Tillie? I can't believe my eyes. What do I owe this pleasure?"

"I'm here to ask a favor. I need your brother's phone number." She went on to tell him about Em's latest episode.

"Mac, Nicole's at her wit's end. She's going to call Tony's family in New York to help her and she should, but she's not comfortable with taking money from them or worse going to live with them as they expect."

"So do you want to call Slade so that he can help her financially or to help get Em to a new hospital? If it's for money I'm sure he would want to help, but the way I understand it, Nicole wouldn't be comfortable with Slade coming into the picture. He told me you offered to help her with Barry Keat's loan and she refused."

"You know about that?"

"Yeah, Slade was really upset with the guy. I'm not sure if Nicole knows it or not, but Slade took care of the loan. He didn't trust Barry, but he was afraid Nicole wouldn't approve of his interference so he did it without her knowing. He figured she couldn't get any madder at him."

"Yes, I assumed he had. I knew he was planning to pay the man off, but I wasn't sure it would go through."

"He did it." Mac chuckled. "I'm with you. I don't want to be around when she finds out, but like he said, he'd rather deal with her, than Nicole having to deal with Barry."

"I have to ask. Are you two okay? Nicole said you and he had it out before he left for New York, but, Mac, brothers shouldn't be at odds for too long. You'll always be family no matter what happens between you."

"We'll be fine." He got up, took a couple of steps, turned around then turned back toward Miss Tillie. "Now that's he's gone, I realize there's nothing for me to be upset about. I guess I was mad because he caused the break up with Nicole. I love that girl. I've always been upset about him opening The Yellow Rooster, but really it's not that big a deal. The Yellow Rooster is the up and coming place in our area, but I realize they're not the only competition." He dragged a hand across his chin. "Slade wanted to sink his money into this lounge, but I guess I was too stubborn to let him come down here and save the day."

"Brothers can definitely be stubborn, but you do need to talk with him."

"I know. I haven't called him yet, but I will. Eventually."

"So you're okay with me telling Slade about Em?"

"Of course I am, but I'm not so sure if Nicole will be. Of course we'll never know unless we try. I'm not sure what he can do on the medical front, but he did mention he was going to talk to some of his friends who had connections. Not sure if he did or not, but he needs to know what's happening here and maybe help get the ball rolling if he can."

"Do you think it would be better if you call him?"

"No, you make that first call. I don't know if I'm ready to talk. If he asks about me, you can tell him I'll answer if he calls me. I'm not making that first call."

She shook her head. "Boys. Do you ever grow up?" With a laugh, she walked up to him and threw her arms around Mac. "My husband loved your dad and you boys when he was alive. He'd be proud of you if you and Slade can help Em, and I'd love you two for life if you do."

Thirty minutes after Miss Tillie had walked into the restaurant, she sat in Mac's car as he drove her home. She felt so much better. Slade would now be in the loop, but she had one more call to make. Nicole was loved at the church and she was sure someone there could also get the ball rolling to get people to help.

Knowing how Nicole felt about being a charity case, she'd be upset, but the girl needed help for her daughter, and if it took a little knock to the pride, well,

so be it.
    She'd deal with her later.

Chapter Sixteen

Three hours after Slade talked with Miss Tillie, he finalized what needed to be done in his office and would soon be on his way to the coast. Nicole might not want to see him, but she couldn't be alone to go through this episode and what it might bring.

Kelli tapped on his door and walked in. "What can I do to help?"

"I think I'm fine. I left you a list of calls to make and a few unfinished projects you can work on. As usual, I feel confident in leaving you again."

"This time I'm more than happy to be here in this freezing weather alone while you're down on the sunny coast. I'd much rather know you're down there with Nicole whether she wants you there or not."

"Let's hope she doesn't throw me out of the hospital room. I want to help that little girl and this is the only way I know how to do it."

"She won't throw you out. A mother will always put her child's welfare first. She'll deal with you later."

Slade laughed. "Yeah, that's what I'm afraid of. Maybe by then she'll forget she's mad at me."

"We can only hope," Kelli said as she walked next to Slade and put her arms around him. With a quick hug and a sisterly kiss on the cheek, she stepped back. "You're a good man, Slade. She knows that. She can't stay mad at you for long."

Slade pulled her into a hug and held onto her for a moment. It felt good to know someone understood how he felt. "Thank you for standing by me." He kissed her on the forehead.

"You do whatever it takes to get Nicole back on board with you because you deserve to be happy, and I can tell she makes you happy." She turned and picked up a couple of folders on Slade's desk. "I'll hold down the fort here, but you promise to keep me informed."

"You know I will. Wish me luck, but more than that wish that little girl all the luck in the world. Maybe one day you'll get to meet her. You'd love her."

"She sounds like a little doll. Now go so you can be with Nicole."

Slade threw a few things into a small carry on. He didn't want to deal with big luggage. He could buy extra clothes if he needed them. With his last minute decision to get back to the coast to be with Nicole, he took the last flight out, one with a long, endless layover, giving Slade much too much time to think. He tried to rest but his mind wouldn't quit spinning. How had he gotten himself in such a mess? Things were going so great with Nicole before she found out his deal for The Yellow Rooster. Now he wished he'd never heard about that lounge.

He hit his hand on the seat rest. The man in the seat

next to him lowered the magazine he'd been reading and glanced over.

"Sorry."

"Having a bad day?" the stranger asked.

"You might say that."

He didn't want to talk, especially to a stranger about his problems. He closed his eyes and tried to sleep, but that wouldn't happen. The only thing he kept seeing was Nicole's face with his business card in her hand. He'd thought about that moment over and over since she'd walked out on him.

If he could take back and redo his life or even that second, he would do it. She was devastated. So distraught. Completely let down.

And it all was directed at him.

He gulped a jagged breath. Now he hoped he wouldn't screw up what he was doing now. With all his heart he wanted Em to have the treatments she needed to let her have a normal life, and if it took his entire bank account to do it, he would gladly give it all up.

By the time Slade landed at the Gulfport airport, it was ten o'clock in the evening so he got a rental car and drove straight to the hospital. For the past seven years he had been in meetings with some of the toughest businessmen in New York, but he'd never felt the pressure in his chest as he felt at this moment. He prayed Nicole wouldn't throw him out of her daughter's room. He was here to help anyway he could, but he had to admit he needed to see Nicole.

At Em's room, he took a long, deep breath then tapped on the door.

"Come in."

Slade's heart fluttered just hearing her voice. He

opened the door and stepped in. Nicole stood at the side of Em's bed looking in his direction.

Slade walked straight to her, dropped his small bag on the floor, and in spite of his resolve to not push himself on her, he pulled her into his arms. To his surprise, Nicole grabbed hold of him and let him hold her close. Feeling her body next to him felt as though nothing had ever come between them, but he knew it had, especially when she pulled away.

"I can't believe you came back."

"Why would you say that? You know how I feel about Em." Reluctantly he stepped away from Nicole. If he'd stayed next to her, feeling her heartbeat against his chest, and having her sweet scent drift up to him, he would've pulled her back into his arms and kissed her until she forgot she was mad at him.

But he couldn't do that, not now, and definitely not while Em lay hooked up to yet another transfusion.

"Is that her first transfusion?"

"No, this is the second pint. For some reason the first didn't work as it usually does."

Slade stepped closer to Em's bedside where she lay sleeping. "Has Dr. Murry talked to you today?" He whispered.

"Yes. He thinks it's time to send her to place for other treatments. He doesn't think there's anything else he can do for her here." She looked up into his eyes. "He told me he talked to you and what you want to do for us. I don't want to be a needy person and take charity, but I'm not going to refuse your help. I'll figure out how to repay you one day."

"That hasn't crossed my mind. Right now the only thing we need to think about is Em and getting her into the hands of a doctor who deals with this illness. This program in Memphis is wonderful and Dr. Murry said they made room for her."

Slade went on to explain everything that he was told about the program available to her. "The medical costs will be taken care of through the program and research money. The only thing you need to worry about is to do whatever Dr. Murry wants. I understand the results are really good with this program, and Em seems to be the perfect candidate to be part of it."

He looked closely at Nicole. Her eyes were bloodshot with black circles under them.

"Have you slept?"

"I think so. I try to sleep here, but you know how it is in a hospital. Miss Tillie stays with her so I can go home to freshen up, but I'm scared to leave her, not that I could rest there without Em."

"I understand, but you can't let yourself get too run down. Em needs you."

"I know. I keep telling myself that, but I get home and can't relax knowing she's up here."

Once more he took a chance and pulled her into his arms. "I'm so sorry I've given you other reasons to be upset. You have enough on your mind. Thank you for not throwing me out of the room."

He heard her chuckle. "I wasn't sure you'd come, and I went through all the scenarios of what I'd do if you came through that door. None of them were good and all of them ended with me throwing you out. When I saw you though, I knew I needed you to hold me."

Her words washed over Slade like warm water on a cold morning. "And I needed to hold you too."

But Nicole didn't stay in his arms long. With a

shudder, she pulled away. "Em will be thrilled to see you here. She's asked about you a lot."

"Then I'm glad I took the chance and came." He wanted to say more. To apologize again. To tell her he loved her. To tell her he wanted to take care of her and Em forever, but he had a feeling she wasn't ready to hear any of that.

"Has Mac been by?" Slade asked.

"Yes, he's come by every morning before work. He brings me coffee and food, then he sends over someone from the restaurant with lunches. I've fed Miss Tillie and half the nursing staff here."

"He's a good man and he loves both of you."

"We love him as well." She looked up into his eyes. "I know the two of you haven't talked since you left, but he wants to. He's not fuming anymore—well, maybe a little—but he said seeing Em here puts things into perspective. His problem with you and The Yellow Rooster is minor in the large scheme of things."

Slade glanced at Em's tiny body hidden under covers and nodded. "You're so right. What's really important in this life always puts other things in their place. As far as Mac's problem with me, talking would be a start. I want to talk with him. I might take a minute and run by the restaurant so we can talk in private. I don't want to do it here. Do you think he'll throw me out?"

"Today? No. Before Em got in the hospital, yes."

"Mr. Slade, is that you?" Em's tiny little voice interrupted what he was saying.

"Hey, Miss Em. It certainly is me. I flew all the way down here again to play with you."

Em smiled, but didn't answer. She closed her eyes

and seemed to be asleep again.

Panic set in. Slade snapped his head in Nicole's direction. "Is she okay?"

"Yes. She doesn't have a lot of energy. Anything wears her out. Dr. Murry said he's talking with the hospital in Memphis and as soon as things are finalized we need to get her up there."

Slade swallowed. "I know you don't want to be in debt to me and I understand that, but I want to get the plane tickets for you and Em and even Miss Tillie if she wants to accompany you, and if you'll let me I'd like to fly with you."

Nicole glanced at the floor. When she looked up, her eyes glistened. "Yes, I'll accept your offer. I have to get her there and owing you would be better than paying high interest rates on a credit card."

He wanted to tell her she didn't ever have to repay him with money. Her love was all he wanted, but this wasn't the time or the place. Obviously she didn't know he'd paid off Barry Keats, and this wasn't the time for that conversation either.

"Good. As soon as Dr. Murry arranges everything with the hospital, I'll get the tickets arranged. Do you want Miss Tillie with you? I'll ask her."

"I'd love for her to come, but she might not want to or might not be able to. Sometimes I forget she's older."

"Yeah, she hides her age well, whatever it is."

"Eighty-one," Nicole threw in. "William slipped that piece of information to me when I made her a little cake and had a few of her friends over for her last birthday."

"Eighty-one. Wow. You'd never believe it. She

looks and acts much younger than that."

Slade took another chance and put both his hands on her shoulders. "Nicole, I know this isn't the right time to do it, but you and I need to talk again. About us."

She looked at the floor again. "No, this isn't the right time. I can't think of anything but my daughter. As I said, I really do appreciate what you've done for us and I'll gladly accept it all on a loan basis, but I can't think beyond that."

"I understand. Thank you for letting me do this for Em."

Slade wanted to stay with her in the room with her daughter, but he knew when his time was up with Nicole. She'd already stepped away from him and placed a hand on Em's arm.

"I guess I need to go get checked in to my hotel. Is there anything I can get for you? I'll come back and spend the night with Em if you think you need to be home."

"No, I've already been home once today to change. I'm fine."

"Can I come back tomorrow?" Slade felt like a child on a playground asking a girl if he could play with her jump rope.

Nicole nodded. "I need all the moral support I can get right now."

Moral support wasn't what he wanted to give Nicole, but he didn't argue. "I'll see you tomorrow."

He reluctantly left Nicole standing in the room. She looked so helpless. He wanted to stay with her all night to support her and to show her how he felt towards her, but he knew she didn't want him that close at the moment.

He'd have to give her time.

After checking in and taking a shower, Slade tried to relax. He flipped on the TV, turned it off, then read his emails and texts, but he was miserable. How could he relax knowing that Nicole sat in the hospital room? Again, he took a chance and at two in the morning he drove back. He stepped into Em's room without knocking, not wanting to wake Nicole if she were asleep.

She wasn't. She sat in a chair with her hand on Em's blanket. Wearing a pink lounging suit with her hair pulled back in a ponytail, she looked beautiful. As soon as the door opened, she turned around.

"Slade, is something wrong? Why are you back?"

"I couldn't sleep and I knew you wouldn't be so I took a chance to see if you'd let me sit with you."

Nicole didn't answer right away and his heart sank.

Finally, she stood up and nodded. "Yes, but I hate for you to give up your sleep."

"It's what I want to do." He walked to the bed. "Is she any better tonight?"

"A little, maybe, but she's not any worse so that's a good thing. The blood she received seemed to give her a little more energy."

Slade concentrated on the beautiful little girl lying asleep hoping the wheels would turn quickly to get her into the hospital in Memphis.

"She mentioned your name again tonight. She's thrilled you came back."

"I'm glad I was able to." He looked at Nicole and could tell she was exhausted. "Why don't we sit together on the window bench? Maybe you can relax enough to get a little sleep. I'll be here if she needs anything."

Indecision passed across her face. Did she hate him so badly that she didn't want to sit by him?

"Or I can leave if you think you'd rest better."

"No, maybe knowing someone is here with me might let me relax."

Slade took that as a positive even though she didn't say she was glad he was there with her.

"Good," he said. "We don't even have to talk. Just sit."

She agreed, but looked hesitant to leave Em's side.

Slade put his hand on her arm. "Come on." He led her to the window bench that had a pillow and a rumpled blanket already on it. He could tell she'd tried to sleep already.

She sat down and leaned back against the wall. "Thank you for coming."

Slade sat next to her and put his arm around her shoulders pulling her to him. "Close your eyes and rest. I swear I'll wake you if she stirs."

Nicole didn't say anything. She simply slumped against him and put her head against his chest. After several long breaths, she closed her eyes and Slade could tell she was already asleep. There's no telling how long it had been since she last slept.

He squirmed a little, got comfortable and simply watched Nicole sleep. She was so beautiful and so natural. There were so few times he'd seen her wearing makeup, and each time he thought how gorgeous she was, but she was more beautiful without any makeup.

For most of the night he simply sat and held Nicole. He was tired, but he was perfectly content to sit all night as long as Nicole got some sleep. Several times he dozed, but was awakened when a nurse came into the room.

One of them smiled at them. "I'm so glad she finally is getting some rest. I don't think she's slept since Em was checked in," she whispered.

Not wanting to take the chance to wake her, Slade didn't dare talk but winked at the nurse.

At five, Nicole took a deep breath and stretched. "Oh my gosh. How long have I been asleep?" She snapped her head toward the bed.

"She's okay, Nicole. She hasn't been awake all night, even when the nurses came in."

"What time is it?"

"It's five."

"Five? You mean I slept almost three hours?"

"Yep and I'm glad you did."

"I am too." She sat up straight, blinked several times, then got up and walked to the bed.

Slade got up as well. His body was stiffer than he could remember it ever being, but he felt good. Nicole had allowed him to hold her while she slept.

She turned to Slade. "Thank you so much. You knew exactly what I needed."

"I'm glad I finally did something right." He stretched. "If you need to do anything before I leave, I'm not in a hurry."

"No, I'm fine now. Let me go into the restroom, then I'll be fine."

Slade went down the hall, found coffee and took it back to her along with a breakfast bar from a vending machine. "It's not much of a breakfast, but maybe it will hold you until the cafeteria opens or Mac comes in with his offerings."

"No, if I'm hungry and Mac hasn't brought anything, I'll have some food sent up from the cafeteria. I don't have to leave, but thank you for this."

He stood hoping she'd throw herself in his arms and let him hold her again, but she didn't. She took her seat by Em's bed. "Again I want to thank you. You've been a lifesaver for me today."

"I hate to leave, but I have to go back to the hotel then go to Mac's. He and I need to talk."

He left feeling better than he'd felt since she'd walked out on him the night they'd made love.

About nine o'clock when he thought Mac would be in, he drove to the restaurant, hating the possibility of another confrontation, but he knew he needed to talk with his brother.

James was the only one at the restaurant.

"Hey, James. Is my brother in?"

"No, sir. Did he know you were coming?"

Slade shook his head. "I got in town last night and didn't call him. I'll wait in the office unless I can help you out here."

"Now that you mention it, there're a couple cases of drinks still on the floor by the back door. I'd appreciate it if you could get them behind this bar. I'm running late this morning and I don't want to give Mac anything else to be upset over."

"You saying he hasn't been in a good mood?"

"That's an understatement. It might not be my place to tell you, but since you left he's been a bear to be with. Then having Mrs. Russo's daughter in the hospital didn't help. He's worried about the little girl."

"Thanks for telling me. Maybe he'll let me give him

a hand while I'm here."

James gave him an I-wouldn't-count-on-it look.

Slade hauled the first case of drinks to where James was working, then when he picked up the second one, the door opened, and Mac stepped in. He stopped abruptly and stared at Slade.

"Hey, Mac. I hope you don't mind me being here. I think we need to sit down and talk again."

Mac nodded then headed for his office. Slade blew out a big breath. *This is going to be harder than I thought.*

After leaving the second case of drinks with James, Slade went to the office.

"Good luck." James said as Slade left him.

Slade turned around and gave him the thumbs up. "Thanks. I need all the luck I can get."

Slade got to the office door, started to knock but realized that was silly. He was still part-owner of this place.

He stepped in. Mac was standing at the small back window looking out.

"I just left the hospital," Mac said, then turned around to face him. "Nicole told me that you're here helping out with Em. Thank you."

"Mac, I love that little girl."

"She said you were going to pay for whatever they needed. That's a lot, and she also said you stayed with her last night."

"It's the least I can do. If I could take away Em's disease as easily I would." Slade grabbed a chair and sat down.

Mac stood a few more minutes looking at him, then sat in his desk chair, but didn't say anything.

The silence was deafening.

Slade sat up straight and leaned toward the desk. "Mac, I'm sorry I caused you and Nicole any distress over how I handled acquiring The Yellow Rooster. I didn't mean to hurt anyone. At the time it didn't seem like a big deal and I didn't even know Nicole. I thought I was helping the owner get rid of a building that was in bad shape." He stood up and walked around his chair and grabbed the back. "If I could do it over, I'd still buy the place, but I'd definitely do it differently."

Mac nodded. "Yeah. I wish we had more do-overs in this life. I'd have a list I could do."

"So do you think we can get over this?"

"I hate that Nicole is hurting because of how you handled the buyout. She has enough to worry about."

"Yes. I know that now." Slade dragged his hand across his chin. He needed Mac's forgiveness as much as he needed Nicole's. "I think Nicole and I can work through our problems. Do you think we can go back to being brothers?"

He watched Mac nod.

"I know you've tried to forget I own your competition, but if you'll let me help, I've thought about ways we might be able to help each other with two restaurants."

"I'm listening."

Slade went on to tell him about bulk ordering and some of the other ideas he had. "I've even thought about talking with Gary and seeing what he thought about giving a share of The Yellow Rooster to you and get Gary involved here. He's the best manager I've ever worked with. He could help us here."

Mac frowned. "Why would you do that?"

"Because you're my brother, and I'm a different person than I was a few years ago. I'm a better businessman and I hope a better person. I know what's important in life. I think Nicole and Em have taught me that."

"Those two have a lot to offer all of us."

"Then will you let me try to make it up to you."

Mac nodded. "Yeah, little brother, don't we always make up especially when you're wrong."

"I haven't been wrong that many times in our lives."

Mac laughed. "Oh, yeah. You definitely have been wrong a lot in our years, but I always have either gotten you out of your messes or have forgiven you for doing whatever you managed to do."

"Okay, you win. But, seriously, if you'll let me I want to try to get this right. If I can work out an agreeable solution with Gary—and I think he'd be okay with it—would you consider working on some kind of collaboration?"

"See what you can come up with. I won't make any promises, but I'll look at what you suggest."

"Gary and I have a good relationship. It's my money that's backing the place, and he's appreciative of that. I know we can work out something."

Slade stood up again. "Mac, you're my brother. Since Mom's not in the picture and Dad is gone, you're the only family I still have. I can't lose you."

Mac stood up and walked around the desk and stuck out his hand. They shook, but then Slade pulled him close and gave him a brotherly hug. "Thank you."

A ton of weight lifted from his shoulders as Slade left Mac. If he could get Nicole to forgive him and see

Em have a normal life, he'd be a happy man, and if Nicole would agree to let him be part of their lives, he'd be sitting on top of the world.

But that might be a little too much to ask for at the moment.

One thing at a time. Em's life comes first.

Chapter Seventeen

Three days after Em had been admitted into the Biloxi hospital, Nicole walked alongside of Slade as they entered the airport on their way to Tennessee. Her emotions ranged from elation of having Em accepted into a program that might save her life to the debilitating fear of putting her daughter into a program that might not work and might actually make her life worse.

Now she walked on her way to catch a plane trying to keep her emotions intact. She glanced at Slade who held Em. He had been nothing but an amazing person doing anything and everything possible to get her daughter to where she could get help. Except for the night when she'd slept on his shoulder, he'd kept his distance and shown the ultimate discretion in what he said and did around her. They were never together outside the hospital room, and he dealt with her only as Em's mother, not someone who had made love with him.

She knew that one day they would have to deal with their issues, but right now he was her knight-in-shining-armor coming to their rescue and she was glad to accept him as that.

Inside the airport Slade found a place for them near the gate and put Em into a seat. "How about a snack before we get on the plane?"

Em blinked her eyes. "Can I have an ice cream?"

Nicole rolled her carryon and sat next to Em. "Is that all you want?"

Em nodded.

"I'll be right back," Slade said. "How about you? Hungry?"

Nicole shook. "No, I'm fine."

Slade left them alone.

"Mama, is it going to hurt?"

"Are you're talking about what they'll do at the hospital? Maybe not. Sometimes though what doctors have to do does hurt a little, but the hurt always goes away. You know how Dr. Murry sometimes has to do things you don't like? This might be the same, but you have been such a big girl through everything you've had to do, I know you'll be just fine. You know I'm so proud of you, don't you?"

"You are?"

"You know I am."

"Will Mr. Slade be with me and you?"

"If you want him to be and if he can get off work."

"Good." Em smiled, laid her head back and closed her eyes.

Nicole tried to relax but she knew that was impossible. She pulled out her phone and called Miss Tillie to tell her they had made it to the airport. She didn't need to do that since they'd just left the hospital, but she had to do something.

Miss Tillie's voice soothed her. Nicole listened as she chit-chatted.

"Slade is coming back with some snacks. I'd better go. I'll call you when we get to Tennessee, and, yes, I promise to keep you in the loop."

Slade sat down. "Is she asleep?"

"Yes, but I know she wants the ice cream." She turned to her daughter. "Em, Mr. Slade brought you a cup of chocolate ice cream."

Em sat up and smiled at Slade and took the ice cream. "I'm glad you got chocolate."

"I knew that was your favorite." He pulled the lid from the cup, then handed her both the cup and the wooden spoon. "I brought one for your mom and for me as well."

"Eat yours, Mama. It's good."

Slade smiled and pulled another cup out of the paper bag he carried. "Strawberry or vanilla?"

The last thing she wanted to do was eat, but Slade's smile was so cute she couldn't refuse. "Strawberry."

She took the cup and surprisingly she enjoyed the sweet cream in her mouth. As usual, the man knew what she needed.

She could get use to this, but she knew she was vulnerable right now and would deal with Slade at a later date—much later when she knew Em would be okay—that is, if he hung in that long. Being a bachelor and never having to deal with a sick child, she was afraid he'd slip away and return to his world of finance and investments the first chance he got.

"Thank you. This is really good," she said. I haven't

had a cup of ice cream like this in years." She took another bite, then looked at him. "I would never take you for an ice cream person."

"Why would you say that? Don't I look like a normal guy?"

"Anything but normal."

"What? You do know that's a hurtful thing to say. It's a good thing I'm not a sensitive guy." With a big smile on his face, he winked at her.

"I'm sorry I don't agree with that. You've shown me you're really sensitive from what I've seen with you and Em. But normal? Nope. You're not anything like the normal guys I've known."

"Explain."

"Normal to me isn't living in a condo in Manhattan or doing some of the other things you do."

Slade stuck his spoon in his cup. "You know that's not fair, don't you? I happen to live a life I've worked hard to get, but when I get home at night I'm just like you and Em or Mac. I pull off my suit, flip on the TV, and eat popcorn if that's what I want for dinner."

Em sat up. "You eat popcorn for dinner? Mama, Mr. Slade eats popcorn for dinner. Sometimes I eat ice cream for dinner, but that's only when I don't feel good. Most of the time Mama makes me eat my vegetables."

"Hey, I like vegetables, but I don't have anyone to cook them for me and sometimes I'm really lazy after I work all day. You're lucky to have a mother who cooks nice meals."

"But if you wanted," Nicole reminded him, "you could eat in fancy restaurants all the time like the one you took me to here."

"You're right, I could, but that gets old too. The more I live this life the more I realize I'm impressed with less and less. Nope. Normal is good."

"I'm not sure I believe you, but we'll see. Em, finish your ice cream. We have to get on the plane soon and we probably need to get to the restroom first."

Slade took the empty cups when they finished and Nicole led Em to get ready for their flight. By the time Em got back to her seat, she was tired and tried to go back to sleep in the chair. Nicole started to pick her up, but Slade stood up.

"Let me get her. You'll be worn out by the time all this is over."

Slade lifted her onto his shoulder and was still holding her when their boarding call was made. For most of the flight he held her as she slept. When she woke up, Nicole held her by the window so she could see out.

"We're flying, Mama."

"Yes, we are. Isn't it beautiful? See the clouds."

Em sat quietly and watched as the world glided by them. Finally she rested her head on Nicole's shoulder and fell back to sleep.

The empty seat between her and Slade kept her from talking to him. He smiled at her when he saw Em had fallen back to sleep, put his head back and closed his eyes. He was probably as tired as she was. Since he'd been back he'd been at the hospital almost as much as she was. When he wasn't there he was helping Mac at the restaurant. She looked at him and remembered how handsome she thought he was the first time he walked into her café. Today he was dressed in the same type of casual business clothes he'd had on that day. Any woman would be proud to have him by her side, and she wished she could have those earlier happy times back with him.

His hands were folded in his lap and in spite of the fact she didn't want to remember, she couldn't help herself. She could almost feel those big hands running down her body as they made love. He'd been in total control, yet so gentle and so concerned about her needs. She swallowed.

He'd made her feel beautiful and loved, and she wondered if she'd ever let herself fall for another man again when she knew it could set herself up for heartache.

She looked down at her daughter, kissed her on her head, then closed her eyes as well. She had enough sense to take advantage of a few minutes to rest before the ordeal in the hospital began.

As soon as they landed, life became a blur. Slade had scheduled a car to take them to the hotel. He helped them get to the room, then took them to eat at the hotel's restaurant.

"Em, I have to go back to New York tonight. I have a meeting tomorrow I can't miss and several other things I have to do."

"No, Mr. Slade, you said you'd be with me while they do that stuff to me."

"And I will. You have a lot of tests to go through and it might take a little while to get everything in order for them to do the procedure. I promise as soon as your mom lets me know when it will happen, I'll do everything in my power to be here."

"Promise."

"Yes, I promise."

Slade pulled out his phone and checked the time.

Nicole hated to see him leave, but he'd given them more time and money and help than she could ever imagine.

"I know you have to leave, Slade. Don't feel like you need to sit here with us."

"Trying to get rid of me?"

"Of course not. I just know you have to catch a plane."

"I'm okay. I have a little time before I have to get back to the airport. You know I wish I could stay, but work calls."

"We know that. You've done more than anyone expected of you."

"Anything for our girl." He winked at Em and she laughed.

Nicole, on the other hand, flinched at his words. His casual use of "our girl" didn't go unnoticed and she wished with all her heart that things were different and Em *was* their girl.

But that wasn't the case.

Slade walked them to their room where he gave Em a big hug and kiss. "I'm real proud of you and I promise I'll be back."

"Okay. Mama, where's Miss Lucy?"

Nicole pulled out her doll from the suitcase, got her settled in bed, then walked Slade to the door.

He leaned against the doorframe. "You sure you'll be okay?"

"Yes, I'm a big girl. Sometimes." She laughed.

Without saying anything, he pulled her into a big embrace. She let him and as always relished the feeling of security of his body around her.

"I'm sorry I have to leave you here. I tried to change the meeting, but I guess I'm not as influential as I think I am."

"Oh, no. You're influential. Don't ever think differently." She pulled away. "I'll text you when I find out if and when the procedure can be scheduled, and, Slade, you've done so much for us already, please don't feel you have to be here. I know you have a life in New York."

"Yes, I do. I have a busy life, but I can't imagine anything keeping me away from being with Em. I promised her."

Without a kiss that she longed for, he stepped away. "Hang in there, Nicole. Em will be okay."

He waved and she watched him walk away wishing more than anything he could stay with her.

For the next three days Nicole stayed with Em as she went through test after test. Sometimes Em would squeeze her eyes and let them do what needed to be done. Sometimes she cried. It was at those times Nicole felt crushed and helpless beyond words and longed to have Slade by her.

Today Em didn't have anything scheduled. The doctors wanted her to rest while they readied everything for her procedure tomorrow. When she fell asleep holding Miss Lucy, Nicole slipped out the room and headed for a vending machine. After telling the floor nurse that she'd be gone for a few minutes, she caught the elevator.

Nicole leaned against the hand rails inside the elevator, but what she felt like doing was curling up on the floor and turning the lights out. Her nerves were shot so instead of going straight to the drink machines, she took a turn and headed for the hospital chapel.

No one else was in the room. She closed the door behind her and sat on the back row. With her eyes shut she let the quietness surround her.

Her body felt numb. So much had happened in such a short time she wasn't sure she even remembered everything that had taken place. Slade had come through for her daughter just as he said he'd do, but she wondered if he'd actually come back for the procedure.

Nicole didn't want to need him. She didn't want to need anyone, but the feeling of being totally alone weighed down on her shoulders.

She raised her eyes to heaven and smiled. She wasn't alone.

Please, please, watch over Em tomorrow. I'm so afraid.

Crying was not part of her life, not since Slade had held her in her kitchen after that hospital scare when she let the tears fall. Today she couldn't hide them. She put her head down in her hands and sobbed.

She wasn't even sure why she was crying. This procedure could be the turning point in her life. Em had a chance at a normal life if it was successful.

So why cry?

Swiping the tears away, she crossed her arms in front of her body and held herself tightly. Maybe she was falling apart. Maybe she wasn't ready to face the fact that the procedure might not work at all.

Then what?

Would she lose her daughter as she'd lost Tony?

No. She wouldn't think that way.

Chapter Eighteen

Nicole left the chapel, got a drink from a vending machine, then caught the elevator back to the pediatric ward feeling a lot better. As she stepped out and headed down the hallway, she froze. Her mom and stepdad stood outside of Em's door talking to a nurse.

"Mom?" Nicole bit her lip and threw herself into her mother's arms. "You're here. How?"

Her mother squeezed her hard in a big hug, then stepped away. "It was easy. A limo came to the house and drove the three hours here. I've never had such a comfortable ride in my life."

"A limo? What? I don't understand." But as soon as she said the words, she knew the answer. Slade.

"Honey, your Mr. Larson arranged everything for Henry and me. We haven't met him but he made sure everything was arranged. Maybe we should've told you we were coming, but we wanted to surprise you and to make sure we would actually get here. It was hard to believe a complete stranger would do this for us."

She couldn't believe that Slade had actually done this either, but then why wouldn't he? He had arranged everything else for her.

"I'm so glad the both of you are here." She hugged her mother again.

"We weren't sure our car would make the trip so when Mr. Larson called us, we jumped at the chance to be with the two of you."

"Mrs. Russo," the nurse cut in, "we've been checking on Em and she didn't even know you left the room."

Nicole thanked her, then turned to her stepdad. "Thank you for coming with Mom. Has Em seen you two?"

"No, she's still sleeping and we didn't want to wake her."

She took both their hands. "I think it's time she sees her grandparents."

"Speaking of grandparents," her mother asked. "What about Tony's parents?"

"I called them. Tony's dad said he was trying to get down. Who knows? Slade may be flying them here as well."

"Oh, Nicole, I hope so. Wouldn't it be wonderful if Em had all of her grandparents here?"

Overwhelmed with what Slade had done, she led them into Em's room thrilled she'd have her family and maybe Tony's family with her during the procedure.

But would Slade get back in time?

Maybe going back to work was his way of letting her know using his money to get everyone here was his way of saying goodbye. Maybe the man came to his senses and realized using his bank account was easier than getting more involved than he already was. Her life with a sick child was much too complicated. She couldn't blame him. He was a bachelor living a dream life. Why would he want to give that up?

How would she feel if he never came back? She'd been so furious about his keeping the purchase of The Yellow Rooster a secret, she didn't think she'd ever want him in her life, but she knew she loved him even when she was furious with him. Now after seeing how he'd put his life on hold to come to the hospital and then getting her parents here, she knew he was a good man.

Slade Larson might not have been completely truthful with her about the restaurant, but he didn't actually lie. He simply never told her it was his company who had bought the business from her.

Could she ever forgive him for that?

Maybe she already had.

~

That night both of Tony's parents walked into Em's room. Nicole had only seen them twice since the wedding, once being at Tony's funeral in New York, but she'd recognize them anywhere. Tony had gotten his dark, good looks from his dad and as soon as she saw them a wave of nostalgia swept over her. Hugging them was like having Tony here with her.

"I'm so glad both of you could come. I was afraid you couldn't get here."

"At the insistence of Mr. Larson," Mrs. Russo said, "we rearranged a few obligations and took him up on his offer to fly us here."

Mr. Russo spoke up. "I told the man we would pay

for our own fare, but he insisted. I hope he gets here. We'd like to meet him and thank him in person."

"Mama, are those people my grandparents too?"

Nicole took Mrs. Russo's hand. "Come see your granddaughter. She's excited to meet you now that's she's older. She was too young at the funeral to remember you."

Nicole stood back and watched the reunion of Tony's parents with their beautiful granddaughter. Unshed tears burned her eyes. She wished Tony would be here to see his parents with his daughter.

She introduced the Russos to her mom and stepdad, and then they all settled down for the evening, trying to keep Em from being too scared about the procedure in the morning. Nicole knew it was helping her as well, but she couldn't keep from looking at the door hoping that Slade would walk through.

Now more than ever she wanted him by her side.

Right at dusk, one of the nurses stepped into the room and called Nicole to the door. Nicole panicked. Maybe they'd decided not to do the procedure.

She hurried to her and stepped in the hallway so Em wouldn't hear if the news wasn't good.

"Mrs. Russo, we're having a light snow fall right now. I'm not sure how long it will last, but if you'd like to take Em downstairs for a few minutes, there's a nice covered back patio with heaters burning. A lot of our parents are taking the children down to see the snowflakes."

"Oh yes. Em has never seen snow."

"Just bundle her up, and of course don't let her get wet."

Nicole rushed back into the room unable to contain

the smile on her face. "Em, we have a surprise for you. If your grandparents will follow us, we have to go downstairs for a few minutes."

"A surprise? Is it Mr. Slade?"

Nicole's heart sank. "No, but it's almost as good."

She whispered to her mom what was happening and together they all caught the elevator. Mr. Russo carried Em and her stepdad pushed the IV stand. As soon as Nicole stepped onto the patio she heard excited chatter from about twenty children who were with their parents or nurses. Some were held and several sat in wheelchairs, but they all were facing the outside where big, beautiful snowflakes were falling.

"Mama, what is it? What's the surprise?"

"Look, honey, look at the sky. That's snow falling."

"Snow?" Em sat up straight in his grandfather's arms. "I want to touch it."

Nicole took her from her father-in-law then carried her to the edge of the patio and let her stick out her hand.

She shrieked. "It's wet. It's snow. It's beautiful."

"It is, isn't it?"

Nicole's mom walked up to them. "If you and your mother can ever get to our house during the winter, you might be able to play in snow and build a snowman?"

"Really? Really, Mama? I can build a snowman?"

Nicole hated making promises to her she might not be able to keep, but she couldn't deny her happiness. "One day I really want to get you to Grandma's house and if we're lucky, it will be snowing."

Em stuck out her hand again, let some flakes fall on it, then brought it to her mouth. She giggled. "I ate snow."

"Yes, you did. Do it again and then we have to get back to the room. We don't want you to get a cold. You can watch the snowflakes from the window."

For several hours, Em stood on the window bench in her room watching the snow. Finally it almost stopped and Nicole tucked her back into the bed.

When everyone left, Nicole crawled in the bed and snuggled against Em. After reading a story to her and saying her prayers, she tried to get her to go to sleep. Em closed her eyes but Nicole knew she wasn't asleep. Her little fingers twirled Nicole's hair.

Finally Nicole saw her peek through one eye. "Is it okay to talk?" Em whispered.

"It is if you want to."

Both of her eyes popped open. "I liked seeing my new grandparents. Do you think Miss Tillie would like them?"

"Of course she would."

"Do you think Mr. Slade will like them?"

"Certainly. He's the one who talked with them on the phone and got them here. He'll love them."

"They'll love him too, just like I do. Do you love him too, Mama?"

"I really like Mr. Slade. He's a very nice man."

"He'd make a good daddy, wouldn't he?"

Nicole swallowed. "I guess, but as I've always said, he's a busy man."

"He'll get here. He told me he would." Em reached over and hugged Nicole. "I love you, Mama, and I love Mr. Slade. I wish he could've seen the snow too."

"I think Mr. Slade is seeing his own snow in New York. Now try to get some sleep."

"Stay by me tonight." Em closed her eyes and

seemed to fall asleep almost immediately.

Slade had not called but had texted her he was trying to get away from New York. She hoped he could find a flight that wasn't cancelled because of the snow. She didn't want her daughter to go into the procedure without him here. He'd made a promise to her little girl.

At two o'clock in the morning Nicole moved to the window bench when the shift nurse came in. The snow had stopped, but lights in the parking lot showed a thin coating on top of cars below her. She was glad that Em had gotten to see it earlier, but hoped it wasn't so bad that Slade's plane was cancelled.

At four-thirty she was still awake, tossing and turning, and praying for her daughter's well-being. The door opened. Nicole glanced up expecting to see a nurse but instead, Slade eased his body through the door.

Nicole threw the covers off and hurried to him. He opened his arms and she fell into them. She held him tightly, then raised her head and kissed him. Slade groaned and kissed her back.

"When did you get in?" Her heart pounded but she managed to get the words out when she finally pulled away.

"About midnight, but I didn't want to disturb you."

"I'm so glad you're here. It's the last thing Em talked about before she fell asleep."

"I tried to get an earlier flight, but that one was cancelled because of snow in Atlanta. I was lucky to get another flight that stopped over in Memphis. I fly so much with this airline that they helped me change flights."

"I'm thrilled that you're here now." She kissed him

again. "I didn't know how much I missed you."

He caressed her face. "Not as much as I missed you. Now tell me how she's doing."

They walked to her bedside, then Slade ran his hand softly through Em's. "I've been worried about her, but she looks pretty good. Is she scared?"

"She is, but she's been her usual upbeat self."

"Did your parents and in-laws get here?"

"Of course they did. They had a Larson travel agency making sure they got here. Slade, I can't believe you did all that. You have spent way too much money on us."

Slade touched her lips with his fingers. "I don't want you to say that. There's no price to be put on that little girl's happiness. She needed to have her grandparents here, and I wanted to make sure they were here for you as well."

"And you. Em has told me over and over you'd be here because you promised her."

"Believe me. I would never have broken that promise."

"Thank you. I owe you my life."

"I'll remind you of that one day." He laughed.

"No, I'm serious. I'm not sure how we would've done all this alone."

For the next hour she cuddled next to him on the window bench not believing he was actually here with her. Just having him by her gave her the strength to face what her daughter was going to go through. Was she a weakling and needed a man by her or was she in love with Slade and simply wanted him?

Em had asked her if she loved Slade and she didn't know how to answer her daughter. Right at this moment though she thought she knew the answer, but just having his arms around her was enough right now. She'd answer those questions after Em's procedure.

By five-thirty nurses started coming in to get Em ready. She and Slade stepped in the hall. When the first nurse left, they reentered the room and Slade walked up to her bed. "I told you I'd get here."

"Mr. Slade." She sat up and threw her arms around his neck. "Mr. Slade I saw snow last night. It snowed and I got to touch it and even eat it."

"Man, that's a wonderful surprise. I saw snow in New York and I touched it too."

"You weren't here but it was the same snow with me and with you." She looked at Nicole. "Now I'm ready. Mr. Slade is here."

And so was the hospital. Within thirty minutes Em had been given a light sedative and by the time her grandparents got to the room, she was asleep. Both sets of grandparents, Slade, and Nicole huddled together and followed several nurses wheeling a sleeping Em down the hall.

When they could go no farther, Nicole leaned down and kissed her one more time then looked up at the nurse. "Please take care of her."

"You know we will. She has the best doctors around."

As the double doors to Surgery closed, Nicole's legs almost gave out. She slumped against Slade who held her tightly against him.

"She'll be fine, Nicole."

Nicole nodded and let Slade lead her to the surgery waiting room. Two other young parents and families sat together, some holding hands, some leaning on someone else. At the moment she had Slade and her parents and in-laws and didn't feel alone anymore.

They found seats and Slade sat next to her. No one said anything as they tried to pass the time. Every time the phone rang to give the receptionist information, Nicole sat up hoping it would be about Em. Finally at the end of the first hour, the call was about Em. The receptionist talked, then called for someone in the Russo family. Slade followed her to the desk.

"The procedure is still going on but is going well, and your little girl is doing great," The receptionist explained. "It should be about another hour before you'll be able to see her in recovery, but we'll let you know when the procedure is over. The doctor will meet you for a short conference."

Joy filled Nicole's heart and tears filled her eyes. "Thank you. Thank you so much."

The good news put everyone at ease and for the first time, the family talked. Slade never left her side. She couldn't have asked for better support. Slade was comfortable with the group and seemed relaxed even around Tony's parents.

Nicole wondered what they thought about her having a man with her. She hoped they approved because ever since Slade walked through the door to Em's room this morning, she knew she felt complete with him by her side.

"You okay?" Slade sat next to her. All the others were either at the coffee stand or in the restroom.

"I am now that the news is good and, of course, that you're here." She took his hand.

"You're trembling."

She looked down at her hand in his. "I think I've

been shaking since they took Em away." She pulled in a long jagged breath. "I can't wait to see her."

"Another hour. We'll get through this. Together."

Slade looked so sincere when he said things like that. Was she reading too much into his words? She wanted them to be together—all of them. Was she a bad person to hope for happiness with Slade when her daughter was still in surgery?

"You're in deep thought. Want to share?" Slade interrupted her momentary escape into what she hoped wasn't fantasy land.

She shook her head. "If I say the words, I might jinx it."

He chuckled low.

Before she felt obligated to tell him anything, the grandparents came in and sat back down.

"Any more word from surgery?" her father-in-law asked.

"No, just the latest when you were here and told us things were going well." She glanced at her phone. "We should be called back soon."

And they were. She and Slade walked to a small conference room where her doctor came in and reported everything went well.

"We want to keep her here for observation for a few days, then she can go home. She did great and we think her body will start functioning much more efficiently to produce the blood she needs."

Nicole stood up and shook his hand and thanked him.

After a few more questions, the doctor shook both their hands. "You two have a beautiful daughter and she'll be home with you shortly."

Neither Slade nor Nicole said anything. She had been clear that it was Tony who had passed on the gene that gave her the disease, but she was sure this doctor had so many patients he couldn't remember all of their personal history.

Slade stayed with her throughout the next half-hour of waiting, then went into the recovery room with her. The nurses, too, assumed Slade was her father and Nicole wasn't about to tell them differently. When Em woke up, Nicole wanted her to see Slade at her bedside.

For the rest of the day the entire family stayed with Em. She slept most of the day, but clung to Nicole and Slade when she was asleep. Before the grandparents left, Slade asked them to stay in the room. He wanted to take Nicole to the cafeteria alone.

They found a table in the corner away from everyone else. At Slade's insistence Nicole ordered a huge plate of roast and mashed potatoes and gravy.

"You need a little comfort food," he said.

"This isn't a little. It's enough to feed an army."

He laughed. "I'm hungry enough to eat for an entire army."

They ate and talked about light subjects, but when they finished Nicole watched Slade lean back in his chair. His face was serious.

"Nicole, I have to catch a flight out tonight."

She was disappointed, but smiled. "I understand. You've done so much and sacrificed so much for us, I can't expect you to do more."

"But it's not what I want to do. I'd much rather be here and fly back with you to the coast. Your parents have agreed to fly with you and to get you settled. They're excited to meet Miss Tillie and to see Marsh

Isles again."

"And I guess you paid for and arranged all those flight changes."

"Minor details."

"No, Slade, it's not minor. What you've done for us is huge."

He reached across and took her hand. She loved the feel of his skin against his and the strength she found in him.

"For the next couple of weeks, I have to be at the office. We're finalizing quite a few projects before the end of the year, but I'd like to be back on the coast before Christmas."

Nicole's heart nearly burst knowing she'd see him for the holidays.

"I know you were working on the Christmas pageant at the church before all this happened. Are you still planning to do it?"

"I have to see how Em does, but the doctor thinks she'll be okay. I found a substitute who has been working with the children and the choir. If things go well with Em, it would be easy for me to slide back into the program if the church wants me to."

"Then I'll aim for that date to get back down there. That is, if you want me to."

"I can't think of anything I'd like more. Em will love having you with us for the holidays and, well, you know I will as well."

"Do I? I'm not so sure how you still feel about . . . things."

"Things are looking up, Slade. Now that this is over, I have time to think about us and to put my life into perspective." She squeezed his hand. "Please come spend the holidays with us. That would be a wonderful gift for both Em and me."

Chapter Nineteen

It was a beautiful December evening in Marsh Isles. Slade held Em's hand in his and walked alongside of Miss Tillie. They made their way to the church's auditorium for the annual Christmas pageant. Since the trip to New York and Em's procedure, he'd been in New York, but tonight he was back on the coast.

"Hey, Miss Emily, how are you doing?" A lady walked up to them and touched Em's head.

"I'm doing good. I went to Tennessee and met my grandparents."

"I know you did, and I'm so glad you're feeling better."

"My Mama is singing tonight."

"She is. She has a beautiful voice, doesn't she?" The lady turned to Miss Tillie. "And you're looking great too, Miss Tillie. Of course, you always do."

"You're much too sweet."

The lady turned to Slade. "Hello, Mr. Larson. I'm Ellen Thurber. We've all heard what you did for Nicole and Em and we all thank you."

"I didn't do much. It's Nicole who deserves the credit for this little girl."

The lady smiled. "Thanks for coming out tonight. Enjoy the program. If you've never heard Nicole, you're going to be impressed."

"I wouldn't have missed it for the world. I flew in late this afternoon just to hear her."

"And to be with me," Em said.

"Of course. That's a given."

They all told Ellen goodbye. Slade looked at Em. "Let's go get our seats. I want to make sure you can see your mom."

As they walked to the front of the auditorium, several people stopped them to kiss Em and to welcome Slade. He was impressed at the friendliness shown to him and to the little girl. They took their places a few rows back from the stage.

Slade pulled Em close to his side. "Are you doing okay, Little One?"

"Yep. Mama made me take a nap today so I'd be wide awake for this."

"I took a nap on the plane as well. I didn't want to fall asleep and snore during the program."

Em held her hand over her mouth and giggled. "Do you snore? Do you sound like a bear?"

Slade laughed. "I think I do."

The lights dimmed and Slade couldn't believe he was so excited to see a Christmas pageant.

He hadn't seen Nicole for a couple of weeks. It was all he could do not to barge in behind the stage to be with her, but, of course, he knew she needed her time with the children and the choir before the program started.

Still, even knowing he couldn't be with her didn't make him not dream about holding her in his arms and kissing her senseless. He smiled. They'd have their time tonight.

The lights went down and the curtains opened.

"Look, there's Mama."

Nicole walked to the piano that sat on the side of the stage. She wore a black suit and had her hair pulled back. Knowing Nicole, he was sure she'd picked the outfit not to call attention to herself. It didn't work. Slade swallowed. She was gorgeous, and he knew all eyes in the auditorium were on her.

A spotlight came on directed at her. Without acknowledging the audience, she placed her fingers on the keys and her fingers slid across the keys, then the clearest, sweetest voice Slade had ever heard floated across the auditorium. Chills ran down Slade's body. Not a sound could be heard in the auditorium for at least thirty seconds, then several spotlights illuminated the entire stage and row after row of children marched out on stage singing as they walked.

Em sat up straight in her seat. Slade placed an arm around her shoulders and felt as much pride in Nicole and what she was doing as this little girl did for her mother.

By the time pageant was over, Em sat on his lap clapping as loud as anyone, especially when Nicole was singled out and one of the children handed her a beautiful bouquet of roses that he'd ordered.

Nicole took a bow, thanked the children and the audience and smiled in the direction of her family as the curtain closed.

"I'm going to be in the program next Christmas," she said.

"And you'll be the prettiest girl on the stage."

Em threw her arms around his neck and kissed him on the cheek. "I love you, Mr. Slade."

Slade was stunned. A feeling he'd never experienced before washed over him. He swallowed and cleared his throat. "And I love you too, Em."

The reception afterwards was held in a smaller room off the lobby of the auditorium. Em ran ahead of him and Miss Tillie and stood in line with the other children. Miss Tillie turned to him.

"I'll stay with Em if you want to meet Nicole outside the room." She smiled as if she understood his need to have a moment with her.

"Thanks. We'll meet you two shortly. Find us a table." He winked at her and nearly ran out to find Nicole.

But having her alone for a few minutes was not to be had. As soon as she stepped into the lobby followed by her students, parents surrounded her. She did see him, smiled at him, but talked with everyone who came up to her. In between the hugs, she'd glance up at him.

He stood back and watched quietly as she accepted all the accolades from appreciative parents.

Finally, the children pulled moms and dads and grandmothers into the reception area. He pushed himself away from the wall as she walked toward him, but reminded himself for the umpteenth time that he wasn't alone with her. This was a church program and he didn't want Nicole to be thrown out for what he wanted to do to her.

Finally, they came together. He took her hand and

she leaned into him and kissed him lightly on the lips.

"You made it."

"I wouldn't have missed it. You look wonderful and that voice. Nicole, you're fantastic."

"I'm a music major. There were hundreds of us in my class and they all sang great."

"Yes, but you're the only one I wanted to hear, and if I have my way it won't be the last time I hear you." He squeezed her hand, looked around to see that they were alone in the lobby, then pulled her close and sneaked a kiss. When she stepped away, her cheeks were flushed. He watched her swallow.

"I've been waiting for that."

"Not as much as I have," he said. "Let's go see your daughter. She's feeling great and loved the program. You do know she's planning to be your star next Christmas."

"And since someone helped us to have a little procedure in Tennessee, she'll be around to be my star."

He hugged her and walked into the reception to share her with everyone else.

Not something he wanted to do.

~

Miss Tillie volunteered to keep Em for the night. After Slade tucked her into Miss Tillie's bed, he turned around and gave the lady a hug.

"Thank you for doing this. Nicole and I have a lot to talk about."

She hugged him back. "Well, you'd better do more than talk." She laughed. "Now go on and enjoy your evening. You and Nicole deserve it."

Nicole walked in carrying Em's clothes. "Are you

sure you want her to sleep over?"

"I wouldn't have it any other way. Stop worrying and go have a good night. I don't want to see you here picking her up until at least nine o'clock tomorrow morning."

Nicole hugged her. "Thank you so much."

Slade felt like a teenager escorting the hottest girl in school to prom as he walked Nicole out to the sidewalk, then together they walked to Nicole's house. Slade hugged her close to him but neither of them said a word.

He took the key and opened the door. Inside they faced each other, but being this close to her alone was hard. He swallowed. "I think we need to talk before the night goes any farther."

She smiled. "If that's how you want to play this."

"It's not." He laughed. "Still I think we need to talk first."

She flipped on a lamp and turned to him. "I think we need to talk too. I don't know if the night is long enough for me to say everything I want to say."

"Is that good or bad?"

"I think it's a good thing." She walked over and sat on the couch and patted it for him to sit next to her.

He sat down with space between them. He didn't trust himself to sit too close to her. He, too, had a lot to say.

"After Em's procedure I had a long two weeks to think alone at night." He chose his words carefully. "Knowing you and Em would get on that plane without me tore at my insides. I wanted to be with you. I wanted to be the one holding Em on the plane and sitting by her in your house. You have no idea how much I love that little girl."

She reached over and touched his hand. "I know you do."

"But not as much as I love you."

He stopped talking to let Nicole absorb what he just said.

She put her hand on her heart. "You have no idea what that means to me. I knew I loved you the night we made love. Of course, you know how that night ended."

"Yeah, I know but I don't want to think about it. That was the worse night of my life."

"I've struggled with my feelings for you, Slade. I've struggled because I know how I feel about you, but I'm so afraid to give my heart to someone who I might not be able to trust."

"I told you I regret the way all of that went down." He got up and walked to the center of her small living area, then turned to face her. "I swear if you'll give me a chance it will never happen again. I will never keep anything away from you."

"Promise?"

He got to her in two big steps, took her hands and pulled her up to him. "I promise, and because I'm making that promise to you, I have to tell you something else." He blew out a big breath.

"Now what?"

Slade dropped her hands, took a few steps almost in a circle then faced her again. "I guess the easiest way to do this is simply to come right out and tell you. I paid off Barry Keats."

"You did what?"

"Nicole, the guy was ripping you off and you didn't need to deal with that and Em's sickness too. I got him to agree to a sensible interest rate, and he took a lump sum."

Nicole went to her window and looked out. "I'm not sure how I feel about that. You did something else behind my back."

"I did, but Miss Tillie and William both knew and agreed I was doing the right thing. We all knew you wouldn't let me do it if you found out. You needed time for Em without the man breathing down your back." He walked up to her and put his hands on her back. "I figured if we couldn't continue to see each other, you and I could agree on some kind of payment plan you could handle, but that's not what I'm hoping for."

She turned her to face him.

"I love you, Nicole, and I want to be able to say that for the rest of our lives if you'll let me."

Nicole straightened up and stepped away from him. "Are you asking me what I think you're asking me?"

Slade chuckled. "Yes, I think I am. No, no. I know I am. Nicole, you'd make me the happiest man in the world if you'd agree to be my wife."

Nicole didn't say anything. Slade panicked.

"Slade, I would love to be your wife, but as I've always said, I have to think about Em. I really don't want to raise her in the middle of Manhattan."

"Who said anything about living in New York? I never thought I'd ever want to move into a house that I never provided for a wife, but if this is where you want to raise Em, I think this house is wonderful."

"What about your work?"

"I told you I had a lot of time to think since I last saw you. I have several people interested in buying my company. I had great hopes that you'd say yes. If you did and the sale goes through, I'll have enough money to help Mac get the restaurant up to par and then I'd be here to help run all three restaurants."

"Three?"

"Yeah. Slade's, The Yellow Rooster, and your café."

"You'd do that for us?"

"I can't imagine anything in the world that would give me more happiness. You know for my entire life I didn't think I could be a father. I never had a role model. In fact, except for my secretary, I'm not sure I even know any couples that stayed together. After being with Em though, I think I could learn."

Nicole bit her lip and when she looked up there were tears in her eyes. "I can't believe this is happening. I never thought I'd ever be this happy again, but being with you has done that. Yes, Slade, I'd love to be Mrs. Slade Larson."

He took a step to her but she held up her hands.

"One more thing though. We don't have to live right here in this house. I simply don't want to raise Em in a city as big as New York."

"I agree. No big city." He looked around. "I kind of like this little house until we have to make room for a baby bed." He cracked a big smile. "I'll especially love this house if you let me get you into your bedroom. Now."

She threw herself into his arms. "You're welcomed to be in my bedroom for the rest of our lives."

When the elevator door had closed on her at Slade's hotel that horrible night, she thought it was shutting out Slade from her life forever. Now she knew she was opening the door to the rest of her life with the man she

loved.
    Life was good.

THE END

www.ingramcontent.com/pod-product-compliance
Lightning Source LLC
LaVergne TN
LVHW011948060526
838201LV00061B/4258